# THE BASTILLE FAMILY CHRONICLES:
# DOMINIC

I0672529

*A Bastille Family Novel*

By Tiffany M. Davis

Paradigm/SHIFT Books

Atlanta, GA

First Paradigm/SHIFT edition, May 2015

Cover photograph: © Wikipedia

10 9 8 7 6 5 4 3 2 1

Manufactured in the United States of America

## BOOKS BY TIFFANY M. DAVIS

### The Bastille Family Chronicles series

The Bastille Family Chronicles: Camille

The Bastille Family Chronicles: Dominic

The Bastille Family Chronicles: Nicollette (2016)

### The Sebastian Scott novels (written as Tee Emdee)

Blizzard

### The Orisha Rising series

Stormbringer

Ironborn (2016)

## SHOUTOUTS, THANX, AND ACKNOWLEDGMENTS

Shoutout to Corregan G. Brown for all things eyeball.

Special thanks to Cynthia L. Wright (@cynthialanel) and Ekaterine Xia (@katjexia) for their input on game development and gaming; and to Sara Hogan, M.D., of the Cleveland Clinic, Cleveland, OH, for the surgical info.  The expertise is theirs; any errors are mine.

Much gratitude to Jamie Broadnax and Black Girl Nerds; Vixen Varsity; and Dawn Gibson of #Blerdchat for the support. #Blerds.

An ear-splitting "Z-PHI" to the Finer Women of Zeta Phi Beta Sorority, Inc., especially Kappa Iota Zeta chapter; the ladies of Ao Katana; Tiffany Yancey; and Stacye Montez: y'all rock. #MySororsAreBetterThanYours

To framily (you know who you are): thanks for giving me space to do this one mo' 'gain.

To my readers: thank you for buying my books and

spreading the word. We are a small yet powerful army.
#BFCNation

Thanks for stopping by.

### Sensing a Trap

Dominic Bastille, MD, trailed slow, hot kisses down the neck and chest of Penelope Duncan, an OB/GYN who worked at a nearby hospital. Penelope--or Nell, as she preferred to be called in informal settings--writhed in pleasure. Dominic worked his hand beneath her back and managed to unhook her purple lace bra with one hand, a move he'd had ample cause to practice since he was thirteen years old. He took one unleashed, full breast in hand and slowly sucked the engorged nipple. Nell's back arched from the bed. "Yes, Dominic, yes," she moaned.

Dominic bit lightly as his hand reached down past the tangled, damp thatch of pubic hair and stroked her wetness. Nell clawed his bare back. "In me. Now." Her tone brooked no argument.

Dominic knew better than to argue with such a firm demand. He reached over the side of the bed for his pants, which were in a crumpled heap. He fished out a condom from a pocket--he always brought his own when he was at a woman's place--and tore open the foil packet. Nell's hand stayed the motion.

"It's okay, Dominic. We don't have to use that."

Dominic raised an ink-black eyebrow in surprise.

"We don't?"

"How long have we been dating? A couple of months now, right? And I've been tested for STDs and HIV, so we're good." She tried to tug the condom from his hand.

Dominic blinked at her rationale. This wasn't the first time a sexual partner had tried to get him to not use condoms, and it probably wouldn't be the last. Still, his Spidey senses started to tingle; Nell was a physician as well, and she knew there were other reasons besides sexually transmitted diseases that encouraged condom use. He leaned in and gave Nell a long, lingering kiss, using it as cover while he slipped on the condom. He parted her thighs with his knee and slid inside her, relishing the warm, heated friction as he stroked in and out. Nell's legs tightened around his lower back as he brought her to a screaming state of ecstasy, then stalked and achieved his own. He rolled over, panting, and lay there long enough to catch his breath. He rose and strode to the bathroom.

Dominic carefully removed the condom--he didn't want to drip anything on the lavender shag rug beneath his feet--tied a knot in the top, and dropped it in the toilet. While he relieved himself, his eyes wandered aimlessly around the neatly kept bathroom. He gazed at the trio of lavender-scented candles on the toilet cover, the lavender and white print of the satiny shower curtain, and the framed photographs of various flowers that graced the lavender-colored walls. He flushed twice, making sure the used prophylactic was on its way to whatever waste management plant or body of water for which it was destined. He washed and dried his hands on a lavender-and-white hand towel, and went to open the door he'd closed behind him, when he paused.

There was a printed chart pinned to a corkboard on the back of the door, a combination of colorful bars and spreadsheet-like rows filled with Nell's neat script. Dominic leaned closer and examined the charts, even as a chill ran down his spine. He looked at the recorded dates, temperatures, and times of day and flashed back to his long-ago OB/GYN rotation as an intern: this was an ovulation chart. Nell was tracking her ovulation cycles, presumably to get pregnant. Dominic checked his watch against the dates on the chart and nodded to himself. Nell was ovulating. Suddenly, her magnanimous offer for him to not use a condom made perfect sense.

Dominic re-entered the darkened bedroom. He retrieved his boxer briefs and slacks from the floor and dressed hastily. Nell stirred beneath her lavender-and-white comforter and stared at him with bleary brown eyes. "Baby, where you going?"

"Home."

Nell came completely awake as she sat up in bed and pulled the lavender sheet up to cover her bare breasts. Her straight, dark brown hair tumbled across her shoulders. "Why are you going home? I thought you were off for the evening."

Dominic pulled on his dress shirt and looked around for his socks. "I am."

"Then what's going on? You usually spend the night."

Dominic donned his socks and slipped his feet into his polished leather loafers. He and Nell had gone to a play at the FOX Theatre in Atlanta, then dinner in Buckhead before returning to her house in Sandy Springs. He looked at Nell with suspicious hazel eyes. "I saw your chart, in the bathroom."

Nell sighed as she brushed an errant lock of hair from her face. "Oh, that."

"'Oh, that,'" Dominic mimicked. "What's up with 'that'?"

"You may be a transplant surgeon, but I know you did an OB/GYN rotation."

"Don't play dumb, Penelope."

The use of her full name got Nell got out of bed.

She wrapped herself in a lavender print bathrobe that lay on a nearby chair and sat in the chair. She crossed her shapely legs and said, "I want a child, Dominic."

"Congratulations."

"And I want you to be the father."

Dominic sank onto the end of the bed. While he wasn't completely shocked, Nell's declaration still threw him for a loop. "Why? I mean, why me? We haven't known each other that long."

"I don't need to eat the entire meal to know if it's good or not. And you have the qualities I would seek in the father of my child."

"Such as?"

Nell ticked the points off on her manicured fingers. "You're heterosexual, gainfully employed, disease free, handsome, educated, intelligent, have strong family ties, no drug or alcohol addictions, and have a good grade of hair. We'd make pretty babies."

Dominic stared at her as if she'd morphed into an alien. In fact, given the surreal quality of this conversation, he hadn't ruled that out. "Pretty babies?" He checked to see if she was joking, but the serious expression on her face belied that hope.

Nell nodded. "You've got that racially ambiguous, Creole look going; you know, light skin, hazel eyes, wavy hair. And I've seen pictures of your family. Your gene pool is awesome."

"Wow." His stunned laugh was a mixture of incredulity and snark. "First of all, Creole is a culture, not a look. Second of all, I've never been mistaken for anything but Black--and don't want to be. Third, there's no way I could be the father of your child because..." he broke off in frustration and rubbed his forehead near his pronounced widow's peak; he felt a headache brewing. "Nell, don't you think you should have asked me first?"

"I was going to, but I couldn't find the right time."

*I can't believe I'm having this conversation, again.* "We're not even in a committed relationship. Yeah, we've been dating, but not exclusively. At least, I haven't." He inwardly cursed at the hurt expression on Nell's face. He didn't mean to let that slip, but she had to know that he was probably with someone else, when he wasn't with her--and that was often. "And I'm almost forty years old. If I haven't had a child by now, chances are that I won't."

"The right woman will change your mind."

He shook his head in disgust. "And on that note, I'm outta here." Dominic rose to his feet.

Nell watched him as he gathered his phone and car keys. "So, will I hear from you again?"

Dominic was completely over how the evening's

once-pleasant turn of events went south, and Nell's audacity. "No."

Nell clutched the opening of her robe tighter around her neck and nodded. "I'm sorry, Dominic."

"So am I." He opened the door and walked downstairs, then out the front door into the humid night air.

## 1.

"So you're swearing off women."

Mark Garrett's incredulous tone was not lost on Dominic as he lined up his pool stick.

"Four in the side pocket," he said, as the tip of his pool stick met the side of the yellow striped ball. The ball rolled and sank gracefully into the side pocket.

"You, Dominic Bastille, who is almost never seen without a dime piece on his arm, who gets more butt than ashtrays, who has a reputation for doing dirt with the fairer sex, are swearing off women."

Dominic raised an eyebrow. "Excuse me, Dr. Garrett but if I recall correctly, you were doing dirt right along with me, pre-Charlotte. And we won't talk about the size and scope of *your* ashtray."

"And you are correct, Dr. Bastille. But this isn't about me; this is about you. "

"Anyway, I have to swear them off. I've had a streak of bad luck for the past three months."

Mark drew his bushy eyebrows together. "Other that Miss Wannabe Baby Mama? Do tell," he drawled.

"I'm serious. Nell was only the first." Dominic's hazel eyes examined the pool table for his next shot. "Seven in the corner pocket." He took his shot and barely tipped the ball in the pocket. "I didn't know her like that to ride bareback, and I was not trying to have her accidentally on purpose get pregnant, and claim it's mine."

Mark nodded. "It's real hard for anybody to get pregnant by accident these days. And she obviously didn't know *you* like that."

"Exactly. And she's an OB, so she knows how it's done. Not that it would matter."

"I'm still tripping on how she played herself, with that ovulation chart. That night was the night."

"Like Betty Wright. But aside from the fact that she was trying to hold my sperm hostage, her 'pretty babies' and 'good hair' comments killed any faint possibility that I would keep her in rotation."

Mark winced. Dominic was very sensitive about his hair, skin, and eye colors, and he resented women who were attracted to him solely because of those features. "Pretty babies and good hair? As educated as she is, she actually said that?"

Dominic nodded. "Yep. A mind is a terrible thing to waste." When Mark snickered and shook his head in commiseration, Dominic continued. "Oh, it gets better. Two in the side pocket." Dominic lined up his shot, tapped the ball with the stick, and sank it smoothly. "So I recover from dodging that bullet and meet this cutie in

Starbucks about two weeks later. We're chatting while waiting for our orders, and she asks me my birthday."

"Why? Was she going to get you a present? Or maybe be the present?"

"I wouldn't have minded, 'cause her body was tight. She was a dancer with Atlanta Dance Theatre. Anyway, when I tell her, she's all disappointed because her horoscope told her she'd meet a tall, Leo stranger with dark hair. I'm a Capricorn."

Mark cracked up as Dominic grabbed his bottle of beer from a nearby table and took a swig before scoping out his next shot. "And then the icing on the crappy love cake was spread three weeks after that. Six in the side pocket." He shot and missed. Just thinking about his next bit of news messed up his concentration.

Mark walked up and selected his shot. "Five in the corner pocket." After making his shot, he straightened and walked around to the opposite side of the pool table. "So what happened? Three in the side pocket." The solid red ball rolled into the side cup with ease.

"Atlanta Transplant Consortium has a new Director of Media Relations: Cecily Porter."

Mark paused just as he was about to shoot. He straightened and stared at Dominic in shock. "Cecily Porter? As in..."

Dominic nodded and sighed at the unfinished sentence. "Yep. In the flesh."

Mark continued to stare at Dominic. "I thought she was still in New Orleans."

"She was, last I heard. Not that I try to keep up with her, but her mom knows my mom."

"How did she end up in Atlanta? More specifically, of the hundreds of thousands of hospitals in the country, how did she end up at *your* hospital? And why a hospital? I thought she was supposed to be some big-shot public relations person. Shouldn't she be in New York, working for a company with a Times Square presence, or something? Or, if she loves hospitals so much, even over at Emory Medical Center?"

"I have long ago stopped trying to understand Cecily's thought processes."

Mark clapped Dominic's shoulder in sympathy as he bent down to finally make his shot. Once the ball sank Mark shook his head again. "Damn, Sin."

"Whatever, Shame. Be glad you don't have to deal with this madness anymore."

Madness was exactly what Mark and Dominic created when they walked into a room, separately or together. Case in point, women hovered around the periphery of the pool table, hoping to catch either man's attention. In college, a girl once remarked that it was a sin and shame for both of them to be so fine, and the names stuck. Which man was Sin and which was Shame was dependent upon the day of the week, and the indiscretions committed. Since Mark's marriage five years ago, the "Sin" moniker usually rested solely upon Dominic.

"Two in the corner pocket," Mark called out as he lined up his shot. The overhead light glinted upon his gold wedding band. He sank the solid-colored blue ball and started scouting his next shot. "Man, that's why I married Charlotte. Not only is she a good, sane woman, but I quickly realized that there ain't nothing in them streets for me but thirsty women with ticking biological clocks and lowered, yet high expectations. Seven in the side pocket."

"See, that's what I'm talking about! Walking, talking paradoxes with babies on the brain." Dominic drank some more of his beer. "Whenever the subject of family comes up and they find out I'm one of six, and I have a twin, I can see baby rattles dancing in their eyes-- right next to the dollar signs when they find out I'm a surgeon. Although I don't know why people think that we six Bastilles are destined to add a lot of branches to the Bastille family tree; I only have one niece or nephew on the way, thanks to Camille." Dominic's eldest sister, Dr. Camille Bastille Paxson, was pregnant with her first child after getting married over a year ago.

"Maybe one of the others will give you another niece or nephew."

Dominic snorted at the thought of the rest of his siblings having children. "Nicollette is my twin, and I love her dearly, but I don't know if she is ready for motherhood. She's still trying to figure out who she is, at the grand old age of 39 and some change. As for Sheridan and Ted, if they can each keep a relationship longer than six months, then I'll start holding out hope. Grant, bless his heart, is a lost cause. He hasn't so much as looked at another woman since Diana died over six years ago." Dominic stared into his beer bottle. "And I don't want to be a father, either." Which is precisely why, unbeknownst to anyone except Mark and Nicollette, he had a vasectomy three years ago.

"Well, for what it's worth, you would have made a great dad." Mark cursed as his next shot stopped half an inch from the edge of the corner pocket. He grabbed his own beer as Dominic sized up the remaining balls on the table. "Anyway, swearing off women isn't going to help any."

"Nine in the corner pocket." Dominic made his

shot and straightened up. "Why not?"

"Because how else are you going to find The One?"

"Well, unless The One falls into my lap, I won't be finding her. Especially if, while in my lap, her fingers try to find my wallet and my sperm."

Mark shook his head. "Every woman is not a gold digger, every woman doesn't want you for just your looks, and every woman doesn't want to have a child."

"Enough of them are. Their mascot is now Director of Media Relations at my work."

Mark chortled. "True, but you have to wade through the fake chicks to find the real deal. It takes time, once you start focusing on more than a nice body and a smile. Hell, it took me almost twenty years to find Charlotte."

"And you almost lost her, trying to draft from the developmental league." Dominic and Mark, who both played basketball at their respective high schools and on college intramural teams, tended to speak of their dating experiences in basketball terms.

"Yeah, well, I had to clear a lot of cap space for Charlotte, and enter a bidding war, but it was worth it to land such a highly regarded free agent. It's all about the championship, and building a dynasty." He fixed Dominic with a stare over the rim of his beer bottle. "So when are you going to sign a franchise player?"

Dominic shrugged. "The draft classes of the past few years haven't been stellar." He walked around the table, trying to find the best angle for what he hoped were his final two shots of the game.

"Maybe you should stop jumping at the top ten first-round picks. You know, the ones that everyone else wants to draft too. Find you a late first-rounder, or a second-rounder. Lots of quality players there, without the drama."

"Whatever. I can't even think about the draft since this promotion, because Cecily has been putting me through all this press stuff."

"Just tell her you're busy. Director of Transplantation means a lot of paperwork and meetings now, on top of your surgeries."

"Cecily doesn't understand the word 'no', and the CEO of the transplant center is a media whore."

"Sucks to be you."

Dominic missed his shot and cursed. "She's been there a month and she already knows my schedule better than I do. And she's been setting up these interviews because of my research, which interferes with the schedule she tries so hard to memorize. All of which give her an excuse to be around me, and I can't blow her off like I want to. She's so obvious; it's kinda sad. My executive assistant hates the blood in her veins."

Mark laughed as he made his shot and lined up the next. "Cecily don't want none of Miss Lori. The Ragin' Bajan against the Creole Princess? It wouldn't even be a fair fight. Lori would drop kick her into the Chattahoochee River."

"Cecily is a lover, not a fighter. She wouldn't risk her face."

Both men exchanged a laugh.

"On a more positive note, my funding came through."

"Whoa!" Mark grinned. "Now that's some good news!" He clinked his beer bottle against Dominic's.

"Thanks, man." Dominic exhaled loudly. "Virtual transplantation training. It's unreal. I thought I'd never get those research grants. Now, if I can just pull this off."

"If you do--and you will--you will totally revolutionize medicine. Whod've thought all those nights of playing *Madden Live* would pay off?"

"Shut up," Dominic laughed. "Well, now that I have the funding, I have to find someone to actually build the simulations. You know anybody?"

"Actually, I might. Ever heard of McIntyre

Simulations?

"No."

"It's a company owned by one of my former neighbors; it does simulations for emergency medicine services, police, stuff like that. They own a gaming subsidiary, the one that created *Empires of Kush* and *Meroë*." He grinned as Dominic's eyes widened in awe at the mention of two of his favorite role-playing games. "You should check it out. It's in Norcross."

"Cool. I'll look into it."

Dominic went on to win the game after sinking the eight ball in a side pocket. The two friends left the pool hall and walked the three blocks back to Dominic's condo in Midtown Atlanta, where Mark had parked his car on the street.

"You alright to drive back home?" Dominic asked. Mark lived twenty minutes away in Decatur.

"The day that a beer puts me out of commission, is the day y'all toss dirt on my grave." Mark pushed the keyless entry button on his key fob.

"Well, you are getting older," Dominic teased.

"And you're three months older than me, so step off, Grandpa."

"That's Grandpa Sin to you."

"Whatever. I'll holler at you later."

"Alright. Let me know when you make it home."

Mark honked the horn as he pulled off. Dominic turned and entered his building, thinking about Mark's warning about not meeting The One.

## 2.

Taryn McIntyre stared at lines of computer code on her flatscreen monitor, hoping that inspiration would strike at any moment. Her personal project was implementing virtual reality simulations for the masses; while VR had been used for the military before, it was not yet readily available for public consumption. Taryn wanted to change that and had been tinkering with the programming in her limited spare time. When she'd founded McIntyre Simulations over five years ago, she started by doing simulation programs for local police academies. Then she branched out into emergency medical services, which led to lucrative local and state contracts. Now, she was stepping up her game and introducing more virtual simulations; which was more money, but also more risk. Her refinements made it more available to the masses, but it took a lot of work.

The vibration of her cell phone provided a welcome distraction. She checked the screen and answered. "Hey, Ryan."

"Hey, yourself." Ryan Cornelius was a mechanical engineer at a major medical device company that was located a short drive away from her offices in Norcross.

"How's it going?"

"Could be better. I'm stuck on the code for this project, and it's a big project, so I'm slightly freaking out."

"Aww. Don't freak out; I'm sure you're doing the best you can."

Taryn rolled her eyes at Ryan's canned sentiment. A lyric from a Sara Bareilles song came to mind: *Head under water, and you tell me to breathe easy.*

"I mean," Ryan continued, "It's basically a video game, right?"

"A simulation is a bit more than a video game, Ryan."

"Don't trip. I'm just saying, as long as people have fun, that's all that matters, right?"

Taryn bit back a sigh of frustration. Therein lay the major point of conflict between her and Ryan. He was a scientist, she was creative. He was all about practical application of his formidable math and physics skills, which allowed him to live a very comfortable lifestyle. Taryn, who was equally skilled in math and computer programming, chose to apply her talents in ways that were both practical and fun. She'd gotten some of the start-up funds for McIntyre Simulations by developing a couple of cult-favorite role-playing games in her spare time, while she worked as a Project Manager in Modeling and Integration at a military-friendly, major technology company in California. She'd explained to Ryan, more than once, that she now spent the majority of her time at MacSim doing simulation programs like she'd done in California; however, he seemed stuck on her humble video game beginnings, which reiterated his opinion that she did nothing but play *Dungeons and Dragons* all day.

"Well, I know something that would cheer you up. How about a nice dinner up at Stoney River?"

"Ryan, I told you, I'm in the middle of this project..."

"Come on, Taryn; you can tear yourself away for a couple of hours. It's not like we've seen much of each other lately."

Taryn bit her tongue at the poorly disguised bitterness in Ryan's voice. They'd been dating for a few months--if you could call it that--after meeting at a sports bar during an NBA game. At first, she enjoyed being with Ryan; he had a dry wit and lots of charm, and he was easy on the eyes. But after a couple of months, Taryn started to experience what she called the downside of the upside: what had initially attracted her to him, now got on her nerves. Charm turned into an inability to connect on a deeper level, and dry wit became a way of pointing out everyone else's shortcomings while ignoring his own.

Plus, Taryn's focus on running her company and her personal projects didn't leave her with much downtime, and Ryan had shown himself to need more attention than most. While she found his company somewhat pleasurable, she didn't see a long-term future with him. And she was okay with that. "Alright," she conceded. "Dinner will be fine."

"Cool. Pick you up around seven?"

"That'll work."

"Make sure to set your alarm, so you'll remember."

Taryn winced. She did sometimes get caught up in her work and would forget things...like dates with Ryan. He'd had to wait for her more than once, and it was beginning to wear on him. "I'm setting it now." She set the clock on her smart watch.

"Alright. See you then."

"Bye." Taryn exhaled a sigh of relief when the call ended.

Taryn's cell phone buzzed again a few minutes later. This time, she smiled at the picture on the screen. "What's up, Sherry?"

"What's up, T-Mac?" Sheridan Bastille replied. "How's the video game coming along?"

"It's a simulation, not a video game, and it's

masterpiece in minimalism."

"Awww. Writer's block? Or is it coder's block?"

"Neither, and not really. I'm just trying to figure out how to amplify the light waves to further induce tactile sensation during the virtual environment experience."

"I'm not even going to pretend that I understand what you said."

Taryn laughed. "I'm trying to figure out how to make people actually feel stuff better, while playing a role-playing game. I want them to think that what they are touching, tasting, hearing or smelling, is actually there."

"See, that's all you had to say. You know I don't speak tech."

"I know. You can barely work your cell phone." Sheridan was one of the ones who had not embraced the technology revolution.

"I'm an analog girl in a digital world. I miss the days of flip phones. They were so simple."

"Technology is your friend, Sherry. Embrace it."

"You sound a lot like my brother, Dominic. He loves technology. If it can be done by computer, he's all for it."

"Sounds like my kind of guy." Taryn racked her

memory. She knew that Sheridan had three brothers, two of whom were surgeons. Two of them also lived on the east coast, with one back in New Orleans. "Which brother is this?"

"Dominic, the baby. He's a transplant surgeon, specializing in kidneys and livers."

"The one in New Jersey? And I don't think a grown man would appreciate being called 'the baby'."

"He can not appreciate it all he wants; it is what it is. And he was in New Jersey; he moved to Atlanta a couple of months ago for a job. If he wasn't such a man-whore, I'd hook you two up, since he's in your neck of the woods now."

"Too close to home, even if there wasn't the small matter of him being a man-whore, as you call him. And, I am dating Ryan right now."

"He's still around? There's no rule that says you can't date more than one person at the same time."

"I prefer quality over quantity. And Ryan's okay."

"You sure about that? 'Cause you sound supremely bored whenever you mention him. I hope that the sex is good, at least."

Taryn got quiet.

On the other end of the phone, Sheridan's light brown eyebrows rose in surprise. "Wait. You still ain't gave Ryan none? Y'all have been dating for what--two, three months?"

"Two months and some change," Taryn admitted. Which was another reason for Ryan's irritation. He'd let it be known to Taryn that he had a rather high sex drive, and she was not helping matters.

"Is there a reason? 'Cause under normal circumstances, you'd have been sitting on his face already."

"Well..." Taryn hesitated, then said, "He has this running buddy who's dating a porn star."

"What?!" Sheridan yelped. "Seriously? Anybody we've heard of?"

"Nah; strictly C-list, straight-to-video, filmed-in-the-garage kind of stuff. And this chick looks broke down and used up, and she can't be more than twenty-five."

"Well, that's a hard industry, no pun intended. But what do his friend's dating habits have to do with you? Did he try to set up an orgy or something?"

"Not with me. But ol' girl let it slip that she'd been tag-teamed by Ryan and his friend once upon a time."

"Shut. UP!" Sheridan squealed in disbelief. "Ryan's friend is grimy, and you know what they say about birds of a feather."

"Yeah. After that little tidbit of information, I

made sure the temple was closed. Who knew what kind of cooties she had? There's stuff out there that penicillin can't cure, and I like my life a lot more than I like Ryan."

Sheridan snorted in derision. "Girl, call time of death on this fake relationship. There is no pulse, no heart rhythm, and all the CPR and cardioversion in the world won't bring it back."

"Ryan has his uses," Taryn protested.

"Name three."

"Well..." Taryn huffed at Sheridan's chuckles. "He's tall enough to reach the stuff on the top shelves of my counters."

"Blah. You have a stepstool; I was there when you bought it. Next."

"He's really smart."

"Blah. You graduated Phi Beta Kappa from Spelman, and you're a member of Mensa. Next."

"And...uh..." Taryn racked her brain for the third item. "I never have to come out of pocket when we go out."

"Big whoop. You hardly go out, since you're usually holed up in your regular office or your home office, working on your projects. And you make more money than he does, anyway. Perhaps I should have clarified, and said three good reasons. But if he's not even breaking you off, then I fail to see his purpose. He's taking up space, and you've never been afraid of being alone."

"Oh, shut up. Wait, here's a good one: he hardly drinks or does drugs."

"Yay, he's the anti-Jeffrey." Sheridan's sarcasm was thick enough to spread. She sighed. "You really need to let Jeffrey go. He was a cocaine addict, alcoholic, and all-around asshole. You're better off without him."

"I know." Taryn knew that Sheridan was right, but Jeffrey had been a part of her life since the third grade, when he offered to beat up a boy who used to pull her pigtails in the lunch line. Then again, Jeffrey used to try and look up girls' dresses during recess. They started dating in high school--until he broke up with her to date a big-breasted girl at a rival high school; a girl that, rumor had it, was giving up the goods that Taryn's virginal self was not. Still, that was a long time to love someone, and Taryn wasn't one to stop loving easily. She shook off the memories and changed the subject. It was Taryn's turn to sigh. Sheridan was like the Borg Collective on the old *Star Trek: The Next Generation* TV show: resistance was futile. "Anyway, why are you calling in the middle of the day?"

"Had a cancellation on a hip replacement, and my malleolus fracture reduction isn't until three, so I decided to grab something to eat and holler at my LS." Sheridan was an orthopedic surgeon in Philadelphia; she and Taryn had been line sisters when they pledged the same sorority at Spelman College in Atlanta, Georgia. While the rest of their line scattered to the winds after graduation, Sheridan and Taryn had remained close. "Don't try to change the subject."

"Fine, Miss Change Men As Much As I Change My Draws? How is...Peter?"

"Pierre," Sheridan corrected. "And we broke up last week."

"So soon?" Taryn shook her head. Sheridan was known for not keeping a man around for long. "You dated him for what...two months?"

"He was getting clingy. You know I hate that."

"Define 'clingy'."

Sheridan exhaled loudly. "He kept blowing up my phone when I was in surgery, or seeing patients at the office, and failed to understand that I didn't have a desk job like he did, where I could goof off and check on my fantasy sports teams all day. And last month, at the Lupus Ball, he got drunk and kept slurring about us having redbone babies."

"Seriously?" Given Sheridan's legendary temper and right hook, it was a miracle that Pierre lived to see their break-up. Taryn sipped coffee from her nearby

Hello Kitty mug. She felt a bit sorry for Pierre, although he should be thankful he hadn't caught Sheridan when they were in undergrad; she would have punched in him the throat for a comment like that. Even as an adult, Sherry was still not above making her point with her fists.

"*Girl.* And you know I hate that!" Sheridan found the term "redbone", which was used to describe lighter-skinned blacks with reddish undertones in their skin-- who were thus deemed as more desirable than some-- particularly offensive. "But what could I expect from a man who pledged, and then dropped out the next semester?"

Taryn almost choked on her coffee. "That's mean, Sherry! You don't know why he dropped out. He could have had family issues, or financial problems."

"He dropped out because he partied too much after he crossed, and his grades dropped. He actually bragged about it."

"Well, he's Black History now."

"Yes, indeed. Hold on for a minute." Sheridan's voice became muffled, then she came back. "Sorry about that. I have to go and check on a patient. I'll holler at you later. Bye!"

"Bye, girl." The call disconnected and Taryn went

back to staring at her monitor.

~~~

Promptly at seven, Taryn stood outside the converted warehouse that was the home of McIntyre Simulations. The balmy night breeze tickled the dark blonde-tinted ends of her reddish-brown locs and made her glad that she'd worn short sleeves beneath the heavy sweater she wore while in the office. The sleeve-length tattoos on her left arm were visible now that she'd removed her sweater.

Soon, the deep throttle of an engine echoed throughout the industrial park where MacSim was located. A red Corvette slid in front of Taryn seconds later. The tinted passenger window hummed as it was lowered, and Ryan leaned down to see her better. "Hey, there."

"Hey, yourself." Taryn watched Ryan's long, lanky frame unfold from the driver's seat as he got out of the car. He was still dressed in his business casual clothes of navy blue dress slacks, a blue and white striped dress shirt, and black, hard-soled leather shoes. He flashed a pearly white grin as he opened the passenger door with a flourish and gestured her inside the car. Taryn gripped the top of the passenger seat and carefully lowered herself into the low-slung, black leather bucket seat of the sports car and swung her legs inside. Ryan closed the door behind her and she had just enough time to fasten her seatbelt before Ryan hopped back behind the wheel and peeled out of the parking lot like it was on fire. They chatted of inconsequential things as they sped up Holcomb Bridge Road to the popular steak restaurant. Once they were seated, Ryan ordered a glass of Shiraz for Taryn and a vodka tonic for himself before turning his attention back to Taryn. "I'm glad you made time for me."

"Hmm?" Taryn perused the menu, though she already knew what she was going to have: her usual filet mignon with creamed spinach and scalloped potatoes, and crème brulée for dessert. Still, staring at the menu gave her more of an excuse not to engage in deeper conversation with Ryan. Not that she had to worry much about that; Ryan was more of a puddle than an ocean.

"I said, I'm glad you came out for dinner. I've missed you." He removed one of her hands from the menu and stroked the back of it with his thumb.

"Oh. Well, I've missed you too, Ryan. But you know how I get with my work. It's not intentional."

"I know. You're very driven; that's one of the things that attracted me to you in the first place. That doesn't mean I have to like it."

Taryn cocked her head to the side and studied

Ryan. "So, you no longer like that I'm driven?"

"That's not what I meant. I meant that I didn't like that you often blow off personal stuff for your work."

"Well, I don't like it when you travel to China for business for weeks at a time, which pretty much cancels any hopes of personal stuff between us for the duration of your trips, but I suck it up."

"At least I tell you, in advance, when I'm leaving and how long I'll be gone. That means I show consideration. And it's not like there's any real personal stuff going on for me to miss."

Taryn's eyes narrowed. "So I don't show consideration?" Her fingers tightened around the stem of her wineglass, although the wine was too good to toss at him. She lowered her voice. "And are you really pouting about not getting sex? High school much?"

"Please." Ryan dismissed her latter statement, but not before Taryn saw his jaw clench. Her comment was more on the mark than Ryan wanted to admit. "I'm not that hard up for sex, even though I don't really understand why you're waiting. It's been almost three months already."

"I didn't know you were marking your calendar." Taryn's voice was colder than the ice floating in her glass of water.

"I'm not. But waiting seems to be a theme with you. Not that I'm trying to bring up all the times you've kept me waiting because of your work, when you showed up at all."

Taryn took a deep gulp of the wine to calm her nerves. She would have been better off ordering a pizza, in her own home, if she'd known that Ryan was going to go full passive-aggressive on her and try to pick a fight. "Ryan, let's not fight. Let's just enjoy a nice dinner, and try to catch up on what's been going on in our lives."

Ryan gave a forced smile." Okay." The server arrived and Ryan gave him their orders. The soft overhead lights glinted on the thinning patch of auburn hair atop his closely cropped head.

They spoke of Ryan's upcoming trip to his company's manufacturing arm in Guangzhou; MacSim's nomination for Woman-Owned Business of the Year by the Norcross Chamber of Commerce; Ryan's consideration of upgrading to the upcoming new model of Corvette; and Taryn's new client, a new medical center in Atlanta that specialized in organ transplants.

"How can they only specialize in transplants?" Ryan scoffed. "Isn't that what Emory Hospital is for?"

"Why not? Lasik centers only specialize in Lasik surgery."

"Yeah, but aren't they usually affiliated with a hospital, for the actual procedure?"

"I don't know, but they're not asking me to do the transplants. They're asking me to work with them on some training simulations."

"I wouldn't trust a doctor who didn't learn his skills the old-fashioned way: by training under another, real, human doctor."

"Well, it could be argued that some wouldn't trust medical devices that were built by robots, or manufactured outside of the United States." Taryn smiled sweetly after delivering the barb; Ryan designed medical devices that were mass produced for dirt cheap at his company's facility in China.

Ryan's auburn eyebrows formed a vee of displeasure. "We haven't had any complaints about our medical devices."

"Did I say I was talking about you or your company?"

Ryan glowered at Taryn over his Porterhouse steak.

The rest of the meal passed with a low-level tension, and Taryn was glad that Ryan called for the check after ordering dessert to go. The ride back to her office was quiet, and Ryan screeched to a halt in front of her building. They sat in silence, unsure of what to say, especially since this may have been the beginning of the end of their relationship.

"I'll call you when I get back from Hong Kong," Ryan said finally.

"Okay," Taryn nodded. "Have a safe trip."

"Thanks." Ryan got out of the car and opened Taryn's door. Taryn alighted and they looked at each other before exchanging an awkward, nose-bumping kiss. Ryan shoved his hands in his pockets, his dark, slanted eyes regarding Taryn thoughtfully before he got back in the car and sped out of the parking lot.

Taryn walked over to her silver Tesla S sedan and hit the lock button on her key fob. The alarm chirped off and the locks snicked back as she slid into the leather bucket seats. "Home," Taryn ordered the voice-activated driverless command as she put on her seatbelt. The car pulled off smoothly and Taryn turned on the air conditioner and lights in her house with a tap of her smartwatch screen, then checked her email as the car navigated the negligible traffic until it pulled into the driveway of Taryn's home, ten minutes away. She tapped the app on her smart watch again and the garage door lifted as the car stopped in the driveway. Taryn grabbed her tote bag and got out. Once the driver's side door closed, the car pulled forward into the garage while Taryn walked to her front door. She heard the garage door lower as she pressed her hand to the palm plate by the door, and leaned forward while a beam of blue light shot out and scanned her retina. The light above the palm plate switched from red to green and Taryn entered the warmth of her foyer.

Taryn slipped off her shoes and walked in socked feet across gleaming pine floors into her living room, where she dumped her tote bag on the couch. She padded upstairs to her bedroom, where she showered and changed into leggings and an oversized "Black Girls Code" T-shirt. She strode down a long hallway to an elevator, which took her downstairs to her basement. When Taryn had the house built, she had the basement retrofitted to her specifications. She exited the elevator and walked over to a door set flush into the wall. She gave her palm and eye to another biometric scan, then walked through the sliding door to a large, white room. She went into the adjacent game room, which was comfortably outfitted, and settled into the captain's chair that faced a 60" HD flatscreen monitor. The chair molded to Taryn's body like a possessive lover, as it should have after having Taryn sit in it for hours on end for the past five years.

She booted the system and picked up her console controls as *Empires of Kush: Meroë*, the second role-playing game she'd developed, loaded. She logged in under her gaming name, Simulacrum, and chose her usual game role: the Warrior Queen Amanishakheto, who was a *kandare*, one of the few queens of Nubia who ruled in her own right, instead of being a queen consort to the current pharaoh. In this game Taryn, as Amanishakheto, had to lead her army against the Roman forces trying to invade her city of Meroë.

The home theatre system attached to the console immersed Taryn--or Amanishakheto--in the sounds of battle: men screaming, swords and spears clashing, bodies dropping due to injury or death. The hoofbeats of horses and camels stirred up the sand as Queen Amanishakheto swung her own sword against the torrent of red-cloaked Romans, their red-plumed metal helmets glinting in the Egyptian sun.

A private message box from the gamer called "Nib-mur-re" popped up.

### Where you been, buddy?

Taryn smiled. Nib-mur-re and she had been both opponents and partners in various games, but he favored *Meroë*, for some reason. She stabbed a Roman soldier through the heart then typed a quick response:

Some of us have to work, you know. :)

After her army defeated the Romans and advanced up the White Nile, another message popped up:

Napata?

Taryn grinned. *Empires of Kush: Napata* was her baby. It was the first role-playing game she'd developed by herself, sole credit, no drama. It was one of the games that help fund what was now McIntyre Simulations. After the legal wringer she went through in California, developing and releasing *Napata* to the masses to a pretty decent reception, was a much-needed ego boost. She even got "One to Watch" recognition from *GamerWorld* magazine. Since the game allowed for individual as well as group play, she and Nib-mur-re had played some scenarios together, and some in a group which called themselves The Alchemists of Kush, in a nod to speculative fiction author Minister Faust and his bestselling book of the same name. Taryn responded to the message:

Sure. Duo or group?

The reply came back quickly:

Me and you. Haven't had you to myself in a while. ;)

Taryn couldn't help but blush when she read the message, and wondered what it said about her that she got more excitement from flirting online with Nib-mur-re, than she did spending time with Ryan. While she shut down *Meroë* and waited for *Napata* to load, she once again clicked on Nib-mur-re's user name and viewed his profile:

**Username:** Nib-mur-re

**Gender:** M

**Age:** N/A

**Location:** The Bayou

**Birthday:** January 10

**Hobbies:** RPG, pool, hoops, slicing & dicing

The profile didn't tell Taryn much; she wondered how old Nib-mur-re was. For all she knew, she could be gaming with a twelve year-old. But the tone of his messages suggested that he was at least an adult. As for his location, she assumed he was in New Orleans or thereabouts; there was no other bayou of which she knew. She'd Googled the term "nib-mu-re" and learned that it was an ancient Nubian word for "healer". Hmm; maybe he was a history buff, or worked in a medical profession. The "slicing and dicing" gave her pause; she hoped he wasn't a serial killer. Not that she was worried; she didn't put her pertinent information in her profile, either, and she made sure that her computer IP address was masked.

*Napata* was up and running. Taryn once again took a queenly role; this time, it was Tabiry, the Queen Consort of Nubia and Egypt, and the wife of the Pharaoh Piye, who established the kingdom of Kush during the twenty-fifth Dynasty of Egypt. In *Napata*, Tabiry was charged with assisting her husband Piye behind the scenes, while he overthrew King Sheshonq at the capital of Memphis and established Napata. Tabiry also had to help oversee the construction of pyramids.

Taryn was not surprised to see that Nib-mur-re had taken on the role of the Pharaoh Piye. As Tabiry assembled the maidens to sew raiment for the army, another private message arrived.

Make sure we look good when we go to battle,

Wife. :D

Taryn chuckled as she replied,

Just for that, we'll deck you all out in plain

linen...Husband. ;)

She continued to chuckle as she settled into the game.

### 3.

Dominic sipped from a now-cold cup of coffee as he rubbed his bleary hazel eyes. He'd been in his office since six a.m. and had barely made a dent in the mountain of paperwork. Years of arriving to work at five a.m. for surgeries had him in the habit of waking up early, but his recent promotion to Director of Transplantation made an early appearance a necessity.

He sat back in his chair with a weary sigh. While it was a professional coup to be the number-two man at the fledgling Atlanta Transplant Consortium--indeed, the director position at a cutting-edge medical startup, plus a much larger salary, signing bonus, and other perks were the only reason he'd left his position as an attending physician at a hospital in Newark, New Jersey two months ago--Dominic missed the days when all he did was surgery. Now, his life was an endless round of meetings, budgets, teaching, research, and politics. His days in the operating room were relatively few and far between, which sucked. He loved cutting, and the loss of doing it on a daily basis ached like a phantom limb.

A brisk knock on his door announced the entrance of Lori Belgrave, his executive assistant. "Good morning, Dr. Bastille," she greeted as she approached his desk with an armful of files and papers.

"Good morning, Lori." He eyed the pile warily.

"Busy week ahead." Her crisp, British-tinged lilt was still prominent, though she'd been gone from her native Barbados for over thirty years. She placed a thick patient file in front of him. "The Board of Directors wants you to review this multi-organ transplant case and see if we can do it here." She slapped down a flag-studded copy of a medical journal. "You need to submit your comments on this journal article by close of business on Friday, so that it can be submitted next week." A paper-clipped packet of papers followed. "These are profile summaries of the first crop of third-year residents from Morehouse School of Medicine, who are doing a Transplant subspecialty, along with your teaching schedule. You're doing Grand Rounds with them tomorrow morning over in the patient wing, after which you are scrubbing in to demonstrate the latest ex-vivo kidney graft technique."

Another sheaf of papers joined the pile. "Your division staff meeting begins in thirty minutes, and you have lunch scheduled with Dr. Winters at 12:30, followed by a Budget Committee meeting at two." She handed him a manila folder. "Speaking of budgets, you have to sign off on these requisition requests." She passed him a blue folder. "These are CVs for you to review for the next crop of residents, and these," she gave him a red folder, "are the CVs for the opening on the lung transplant team. You have interviews for the opening on the heart transplant team scheduled for Wednesday afternoon and Thursday morning." She plunked down a green folder. "You have several invitations to various fundraisers for which you'll need to RSVP by Wednesday. Oh, and The National Institute of Diabetes and Digestive and Kidney Diseases wants you to speak at a dinner honoring Dr. Leman, who's retiring next month. Lastly," she placed two sheets of paper, stapled together, atop the pile, "You meet with the IRB tomorrow afternoon regarding your research project, and you have a meeting at 3:30 today with Cecily Porter and the CEO of McIntyre Simulations to discuss your new project."

Dominic shook his head. Cecily was determined to tax his nerves. "I'm not sure about this project. I mean, learning transplant techniques with what are basically advanced video games is still relatively new, and the way I want to do it is pretty radical."

"You are one of the new faces of modern healthcare. Your ways of integrating technology into the transplant program, especially with the cell phone application that monitors postoperative measurements, has garnered a lot of attention."

"Well, for all that, I'm still a bit old-school. Some things you can't learn by proxy, but the rates of organ transplants in this country are increasing, while the physicians to perform those transplants are decreasing. Something has to be done in order to train more physicians properly, in less time. ." Dominic sighed. "Do I have a choice in doing this interview?"

Lori grinned. "No. A little bird told me that it had been originally scheduled for next Tuesday, here in your office, but she chose to move it up. So act surprised when she brings it up." The slight emphasis on "she" underscored her distaste for Cecily, and Dominic bit back a grin. Lori shook the tension from her now-empty arms and turned to leave. "Don't forget to take your iPad," she tossed over her shoulder.

Dominic tried not to feel so overwhelmed. "Do I get to breathe?"

"Not today." Lori shut the door behind her.

~~~

Taryn's sensible heels made dull clicks across the hardwood lobby floor of the Atlanta Transplant Consortium. She approached the sleek, walnut reception console and gave her name to the receptionist, who had her sign in. Taryn clipped the plastic visitor name tag to the lapel of her blazer and looked around the well-appointed lobby. The hardwood floor bisected deep, navy blue carpeted waiting areas, which were filled with comfortable sofas and chairs against cream-colored walls dotted with artwork. Softly lit lamps and glossy vined plants sat atop walnut end tables, and a discreet coffee station was tucked away behind a partial screen in a corner. Walnut coffee tables were spread with magazines and ATC literature arranged around a fresh floral centerpiece. Classical music piped in through the overhead sound system. Taryn figured that since the Atlanta Transplant Consortium was a private facility, it could afford a more expensive-looking lobby.

The sound of high heels clacking on the floor caught her attention. She turned and saw a slender woman with obvious curves, perfect makeup, and sandy brown, straight hair that flowed just past her shoulders. Taryn wasn't much of a clotheshorse, but she did subscribe to *Vogue* magazine and could have sworn that she saw the same V-neck, dark green and rust-patterned, silk wrap dress by a major designer in last month's issue. The woman flashed a professional, whitened grin as she approached Taryn and held out a manicured hand. "Hello, Ms. McIntyre," she said as "I'm Cecily Porter, Director of Media Relations."

"Taryn McIntyre. Pleased to meet you." Taryn shook Cecily's hand, which was like squeezing a dead goldfish.

"I'm sure." Cecily's cool, greyish-blue eyes appraised Taryn from head to toe, lingering on her gold-tinted locs. "I'll take you upstairs to our conference room."

Cecily guided Taryn to a bank of elevators, navigating expertly on four-inch green leather stilettos with red soles. Taryn's knees ached just looking at them. They made small talk until they reached the end of a carpeted corridor in the same navy blue shade as the lobby. Cecily waved her into a small conference room where two men and another woman were already seated and chatting. They broke off their conversation and the men stood when Cecily and Taryn entered.

"Gentlemen, this is Taryn McIntyre of McIntyre Simulations," Cecily introduced. "Ms. McIntyre, this is Vincent Behane, CEO of the Atlanta Transplant Consortium." Vincent's gelled, cropped, curly brown hair barely moved as he pumped Taryn's outstretched hand with enthusiasm. "And this is Arthur Parker, head of our IT Department." Arthur, a lanky man with a prominent Adam's apple and a mop of blond hair, shook her hand with a shy grin. "Monica Muir, head of the Legal

Department." Monica gave a firm handshake that was in line with her tailored charcoal grey dress and neatly French-rolled red hair. Cecily looked at Vincent. "Where is Dr. ...?"

"Right here." A handsome man swept into the room with dark hair and an easy smile. An iPad and a stack of files were tucked beneath his arm. He held out a hand to Taryn. "Dr. Dominic Bastille, Director of Transplantation."

"Taryn McIntyre, of McIntyre Simulations." Taryn shook his hand and felt a spark, which she quickly attributed to static electricity from the carpet. "Nice to meet you." Dominic Bastille? Sheridan's baby brother? He worked here? She eyed the tall frame and prominent widow's peak that Sheridan also had, and noticed that he and Sheridan shared the same face and eye shapes. The differences were that Sheridan's eyes and hair were brown, while Dominic's eyes were hazel and his hair was ink black. His effect on the women in the room was noticeable. From the corner of her eye, Taryn noticed that the attorney sat up straighter--the better to push out her impressive chest beneath the tailored suit jacket-- and smoothed a hand over her French roll. Cecily scooted her chair closer to Dominic, who sat in the empty chair between herself and Taryn. Personal space obviously meant little to Cecily, as she was close enough to count the hair follicles on his head.

"I rate the boss on this one? Sweet." Dominic grinned and examined Taryn. She was cute in the face, and he was digging her big, brown eyes framed by long, dark lashes. He also admired her shoulder-length locs. He felt Cecily staring at Taryn from his other side, as if she were a bug in a zoo, and bit back a grin. "So, you're going to help us build the surgical simulations?"

"That's why I'm here. When Vincent approached me about the project, I found it interesting."

"Well, your proposal was outstanding, and Bryan Perkins spoke very highly of you," Vincent piped up. "He said you were the best coder he'd ever worked with at SimDyne, and I did my homework. You've done simulations for police and fire departments, and emergency medical technicians, and they've had nothing but good things to say about your programs. Bryan told me that you were worth every penny that you charged. And, of course, your former neighbor Mark Garrett praised you to the skies."

Dominic managed to keep the surprise off his face. Taryn was Mark's former neighbor, the one he'd mentioned? The creator of his favorite RPGs? Dominic resisted the urge to squeal like a fanboy, although he did wonder if she'd autograph his copy of *Empires of Kush: Napata.*

Taryn smiled. "Bryan is a good guy, and I miss living near Mark and his wife--though I don't miss defragging Mark's hard drive every month."

"He's not the most computer literate person in the world," Dominic admitted with a twinkle in his eye.

Taryn switched her gaze back to Dominic. "You know Mark Garrett?"

"He's my best friend, since undergrad."

Oh boy. She and the Garretts were on good terms; if this simulation project went south, it could cause some complications in the relationship. Then again, men usually didn't let business affect the personal like women did. Taryn caught the narrowed eyes of Cecily over Dominic's shoulder and cleared her throat before addressing Vincent again. "And yes, most of my work has been with law enforcement and paramedical professionals. Doing simulations for more invasive procedures will be interesting."

"I'm glad you said that," Dominic chimed in. He wanted Taryn's attention focused on him; after all, it was his project. "Part of my research in integrating the technology we use every day into medicine. With the rates of organ transplantation increasing each year, we need faster, cost-effective, yet accurate, ways of training physicians who choose to pursue a subspecialty in transplantation. Simulations could go a long way toward making that happen."

"What, exactly, did you have in mind, Dr. Bastille?" Taryn removed her tablet computer from its zippered cover and unlocked the home screen. She opened her note-taking app and removed the stylus.

"Please, call me Dominic." He proceeded to detail exactly what he was looking for, while Arthur and Monica jumped in at intervals regarding needed versus available technology resources, legal issues, budget, and the like. Finally, after two hours, Taryn had a better handle on what needed to be done with the simulations. She had already started writing the code in her head, and couldn't wait to get back home to her powerful, custom-built computers so that she could start bringing the sim to life.

At the end of the meeting, Taryn rose and gathered her things. "I've gotten a lot of good ideas to start," she said as she zipped her tablet into its protective carrying case. "I have some ideas for a mock sim, and I'll let you know when it's ready, so that you can check it out. We'll proceed from there."

"When can we expect the first update?" Cecily

said.

Taryn didn't miss the side eye that Dominic gave the other woman, and kept her own face poker smooth. "I should have the mock sim done within a couple of weeks or so." She fished a business card out of her blazer pocket and handed it to Dominic. "Here's my contact information if you have any questions."

"I'll take one of those." Cecily held out an imperative hand.

"Sure." Taryn handed over the business card, though there was no real reason for Cecily to need it. Dominic was obviously the brains behind this project; any specifications needed to go through him, since it was his research money on the line.

Dominic tucked the card in his pocket. "I look forward to speaking with you soon, then, Ms. McIntyre."

"Call me Taryn."

"Alright." Dominic nodded. "Taryn."

Taryn nodded her goodbyes and exited the conference room. Cecily stomped behind her. "Let me escort you down to the lobby." She stabbed the down button with a manicured finger. Taryn studied the closed elevator doors; while Cecily was within her rights as an ATC employee to make sure visitors left the premises promptly, Taryn had a feeling that the other woman was just making sure Taryn was gone--and away from Dominic. Taryn bit back a sigh. She hoped that, for the sake of the project, Dominic would implement sturdy professional and personal boundaries with Cecily; the woman didn't seem to be the type to take no for an answer.

### 4.

Dominic was going over a patient file for a consultation, when his office door flew open and Cecily breezed in. "Knock knock," she said in a light tone.

Dominic looked up from the chart with a frown. "A closed door means 'do not disturb'. And how did you know I was in here, anyway?"

"I was down the street at the pita place, and overheard Lori say she was bringing you back a sandwich." Cecily sat down in one of the chairs facing his desk and crossed her long legs in their customary high heels. The gesture caused the skirt of her pink and gray suit to ride up and expose a healthy length of gym-toned thigh.

Dominic sighed, not bothering to hide his irritation. Cecily was relentless in her quest to recapture and retain his attention and affection. He silently sent up yet another prayer of thanks that he'd dodged a bullet when he broke off their engagement three years ago. "I'm busy, Cecily."

"All work and no play makes Nicky a very dull boy."

"Stop calling me Nicky. When we are at work, you

are to address me as either Dominic or Dr. Bastille."

Cecily raised an arched eyebrow. "Well ex-cuuuuse me, Dr. Dominic Bastille. You never used to mind me calling you Nicky."

"I never used to mind a lot of things."

"What bug crawled up your ass and died?"

"The 'I don't have time for your nonsense' bug." He turned his attention back to the file, hoping she'd get the hint and leave. He looked up a couple of minutes later to find Cecily still in the chair, swinging a leg lazily back and forth from the knee. "*What*, Cecily?"

She shifted in her seat to flash more thigh. "I'm here on a business matter."

"Then maybe you want to pull your skirt down, say what you need to say, and leave me be."

"It's not like you haven't seen my thighs--or anything else--before," Cecily winked and flashed a salacious grin. "In fact, I remember that time we were in the Caymans and..."

"Cecily," Dominic warned. He was not trying to go down Memory Lane, least of all with Cecily.

"Okay, okay," she grumbled as she tugged her hemline down to a respectable level. "Better?"

"Much."

"Fine." She tossed her straightened sandy-brown

hair over one shoulder. The gesture caused her blonde highlights to glint beneath the overhead fluorescent lights. "Have you heard of *Healthwatch Today*?"

"Should I have?"

"It's only the biggest healthcare publication to hit the market since the *Journal of the American Medical Association*. It was formed by both the previous and current president, along with the past editor emeritus of *JAMA* and some health policy think tanks."

Dominic looked over his notes for his upcoming meeting with a medical device company. "Mmm hmm."

"Dominic!" He looked up at Cecily's sharp tone. "This is important."

"This," he held up his notes, "is important. It's for my research."

"Well, this interview may get you more funding." She smiled at Dominic's sudden interest. "I knew that would get your attention."

Dominic checked his watch as he held back his own smile. Cecily knew which buttons to push. "Let's hurry this up, Cecily. I have Rounds this afternoon."

"Okay. This *Healthwatch Today* interview has the potential for a lot of good publicity, and it would increase our institutional profile. Your reputation as a transplant surgeon, plus your innovative research with these simulation things, is what people want to hear about. Speaking of which--how much do you know about McIntyre Simulations?"

"I know that it has done a lot of quality simulations for police, paramedics, fire departments, stuff like that. Taryn McIntyre used to live near Mark, and Vincent has apparently done his homework as well. I checked up on her too, and everything seems legit."

"So it seems." Cecily stared at Dominic with pursed, glossy pink lips. "But is she capable of performing a project of this magnitude?"

"You don't do computer work for a military defense contractor if you're incompetent. I checked out her LinkedIn profile and called some people I knew in California. She has a solid reputation in the area of computer simulations."

"Hmm." Cecily continued to look at Dominic, then shrugged slightly. "Well, it's your research money. But I'll keep looking for other people, in case Ms. McIntyre doesn't deliver."

"More like you don't want her to deliver."

Cecily narrowed her eyes. "What did you say?"

Dominic's gaze was steady. "Did I stutter?"

"I'm just looking out for your best interests, Dominic. Like I always have." She rose in a huff and tossed her hair behind her shoulders. "You'd do well to remember that." She turned and stormed out of the room.

"That's what I'm afraid of," Dominic mumbled as he went back to his reports.

~~~

By the time Friday rolled around, Dominic was glad to see the back of the ATC. One of the advantages of being in private practice was that he worked Monday through Friday only, and got off in time for dinner. He could now appreciate why his sister Sheridan and eldest brother Grant chose that route. At 5:30 Dominic shut down his office computer, wished Lori a good weekend, and headed out to a dinner date with a woman he'd been casually seeing. Maya was going to meet him at the restaurant because she had to leave for another engagement right after dinner. Dominic didn't mind; Maya had been throwing disconcerting hints over the past two weeks so the less he was in her presence, the better.

Dominic was twenty minutes late to the restaurant due to the infamous Atlanta rush-hour traffic. When he walked into Blue Moon, Maya was seated at the bar, nursing something pink in a martini glass. He approached her and placed a kiss on her cheek. "Sorry

I'm late. Traffic was a mess, and the rain didn't help."

"No problem. They wouldn't seat me unless you were here. I'll let the hostess know we're ready for our table." She signaled for the hostess, and soon they were seated at a table in an intimately lit part of the restaurant. Dinner passed with inconsequential chatter, and Dominic felt a sense of relief as they exited the restaurant to a cloudy sky, but no more rain. Maya linked her arm through his. "I'm glad we got a chance to spend some time together, Dominic. You've been working too hard."

"Comes with the new job," Dominic replied. Hackles started to rise on the back of his neck. Something in her tone didn't sit right with him.

"We don't always have to go out, you know. I'm more than happy to stay in. I can cook us dinner."

Dominic remained silent as they walked. Maya had extended an invitation for a home-cooked meal more than once, but he'd always declined. Cooking implied an audition for wife status, and Dominic was not ready for a wife. Even if he was, Maya would not even be on his long list of candidates.

"If I had a key to your house, I could stop by and have a nice, relaxing meal set up for you. You can chill in the comfort of your own home."

*Oh,* hell *naw.* A key to his house? While Maya

wasn't the first woman to ask for a key, and probably wouldn't be the last, Dominic refused to give free access to his sanctuary to anybody who wanted it. The only people who had keys to his home were his twin sister Nicollette, Mark, and his housekeeper. And that's the way he liked it.

Dominic and Maya paused at her car. "Drive safe." Dominic bent down and kissed her on the forehead.

Maya looked disappointed. "Sure you don't want to follow me back to my house? Or I can follow you back to yours."

"I thought you had a previous engagement."

"I can miss it." Her eyes pleaded for him to give her the green light.

*No, ma'am.* "Duty calls," he said with an easy smile. "I'll talk to you later."

Maya pouted, but Dominic wasn't swayed. She sighed with defeat and got into the. Dominic watched her pull into traffic, then turned and walked a block in the opposite direction to his car. As far as he was concerned, Maya was officially Black History.

His cell phone rang as he walked into the three-bedroom condo he bought a month ago. He checked the caller ID, saw it was Cecily, and let it go to voicemail. He also noticed a text from Maya, stating she was missing him already and would talk to him over the weekend. Dominic sighed deeply as he went to his bedroom, undressed, and pulled on basketball shorts and a T-shirt that had seen better days. He reflected on the sorry state of his love life as he walked back to the kitchen and grabbed a beer from the refrigerator. First up: Cecily Porter. After three years and a broken engagement, Dominic figured that Cecily would have moved on by now. She was an attractive woman, and quite intelligent and personable; she had to be in order to rise to her current position and achieve what she had. Of course, having Alain J. Porter, M.D., esteemed cardiothoracic surgeon and chairman *emeritus* of the Porter Foundation for Medical Advancement, as a father helped to smooth any rough spots.

Dominic shook his head as he plopped down on his leather couch and turned on the TV. Cecily's single-minded focus was once attractive to Dominic but now, it just made him want to do a Usain Bolt in the opposite direction. Even moving to Atlanta apparently wasn't enough to keep Cecily out of his life. Short of hiring a hitman, or getting married himself, he couldn't figure out how to get Cecily to leave him alone. He channel surfed until he found a *Martin* marathon, then settled in to watch as his thoughts turned to recent problem number two: Maya.

He'd met Maya over a month ago at an Urban League fundraiser. She caught his attention with her wit and obvious intelligence, and her rather impressive hips sealed the deal for him. For all of her prowess as an employment law attorney, Maya was surprisingly insecure. What had started as something light and easy quickly morphed into Maya attempting to take liberties where Dominic had granted none. The beginning of the end was when Dominic found a box of tampons beneath the sink in his master bathroom; he knew he hadn't put him there, they weren't there before he started dating Maya, and even his sisters didn't leave their personal hygiene products behind after a visit. Maya started more territory-marking behaviors, like accidentally on purpose leaving behind articles of clothing and makeup on the few occasions she spent the night, and even food. A hint for drawer and closet space was the penultimate straw, and tonight's request for a key was the final nail in their relationship coffin.

Not that he saw marriage in his foreseeable future, much to his mother's chagrin. Of his five brothers and sisters, only two had been married: his eldest brother, Grant, and most recently his eldest sister, Camille. Unfortunately, Grant's wife died over six years ago in a car accident, and he remained a widower. Camille and her husband Andrew had only been married just over a year. The rest of his siblings, himself included, hadn't found relationships that stood the test of time. Being healthcare professionals in demanding roles--in addition to Grant, Camille, and Sheridan, Nicollette was also a surgeon, specializing in fetal and maternal medicine. His brother Theodore--or Ted, as he was usually called--was a nurse who ran a large critical care department. None of their professions left much time to nurture relationships.

Then again, did he really want to be married? Sometimes, he preferred to maintain his bachelor existence. His money, accomplishments, and looks guaranteed no shortage of companions; all he had to do was pick and choose. He could up and travel on a moment's notice, not having so much as a goldfish to think about. He had no worries, even with his rather stressful promotion. But there were also times when he would have liked to come home to someone--the same someone--after a long day. His condo seemed so empty sometimes. He was house-hunting in his spare time but as he visited open houses and pored over the listings in the real estate apps on his phone, he wondered what the point was. Granted, real estate was never really a bad investment. However, for his lifestyle, a condo was more than sufficient, and it was near the transplant center. His contract with ATC was for five years; who's to say whether or not he'd want to stay around after that time was up? Houses were for people who wanted to put down roots and start families. He was not sure of the former and definitely didn't want the latter; at almost forty years old, he probably should have figured it out by now.

Then he'd spend some time with Mark and Charlotte, or Camille and Andrew, and see how good life could be with the right person. He didn't even have to look that far: his parents were a rather uncommon match of people with the "right" backgrounds, who actually liked and loved each other. After his botched engagement to Cecily, Dominic knew that he'd given up on finding such a match for himself. He hadn't shut down, per se, but he was just wary. His superficial dating style ensured that no one got close enough to hurt him again.

He booted up his video game system and loaded one of his favorite role-playing games, *Empires of Kush: Napata*. Though it came out around five years ago, and had spawned two sequels-- *Empires of Kush: Meroë* and *Empires of Kush: Axum Rising*--he preferred the original installment of the trilogy. He selected his favorite role of the Pharaoh Piye, the leader of Kush during the twenty-fifth dynasty of Egypt, and started building his army when he checked the white buddy box in the lower right corner of his large, wall-mounted flatscreen TV. He saw that Simulacrum was online as well; maybe she'd be up for a game of *Napata*, since they'd paired together in the game before. Before he could finish typing his message, he received one from her:

Shouldn't you be out on a date? :)

Dominic smiled and replied,

Been there, done that, ditched the date and came home. Rather play with you.

Okay, that didn't quite come out the way he'd wanted but before he could clean it up, Simulacrum shot back,

That could be taken so many ways. ;)

Dominic let out a bark of laughter. Simulacrum never disappointed in their interactions. He wrote back:

I know where my mind is, but let me know what's on yours? :D

Seconds later:

Just play the game, Pharaoh Flirty. LOL

Dominic chuckled as he ordered slaves to build pyramids in the hot desert. On a lark, he re-opened

Simulacrum's profile:

>   **Username:** Simulacrum
>
>   **Gender:** F
>
>   **Age:** N/A
>
>   **Location:** OTP
>
>   **Birthday:** May 5
>
>   **Hobbies:** computers, RPG, reading, swimming

He wondered what she was like in real life; too often, the internet provided a level playing ground--no pun intended--for those who lacked social skills offline. That being said, Simulacrum could be "catfishing", or putting up a fake profile. Although from the vagueness of her profile, what she had listed was probably true. And although he tried to find out what "OTP" stood for, the most he could come up with was the phrase "outside of the perimeter", which was applicable to those cities outside of I-285 in the Atlanta, Georgia area. Could Simulacrum actually live in the Atlanta area? For all Dominic knew, if that were indeed the case, he could have passed her on the street already. Or stood behind her in line at a local coffee shop. Drove past her on the expressway. The thought excited him before he shut it down. "Let it go, Nick," he said aloud before he hunkered down to the game. Reality tended to suck a lot more than fantasy; for now, he'd just enjoy their online relationship. It was safer that way.

~~~

Saturday found Dominic at his favorite video game store. It was one of the relative few, independently owned stores in the country. He preferred to patronize indie stores over chains whenever possible, although his resolve was usually tested when the chains offered steep discounts on his favorite titles. People were usually surprised when they discovered that he was a big video game buff, especially role-playing games. They relaxed him and got him out of his head for the few precious hours it took for him to complete a playing scenario. He also enjoyed his network of online gaming buddies-- especially Simulacrum.

While browsing, his eye was drawn to the "New Releases" display. He walked over and removed one of the games from the pyramid stack and read the blurb on the back. *Chieftain's Rise* was an RPG where a young man in Africa learned that he was the illegitimate heir to a chiefdom in a large village. He had to fight his way across a wide swath of land, and fight off both renegade warriors and the current chief's army, in order to claim his rightful throne and win the hand of the beautiful eldest daughter of the old chief. He looked at the company logo and saw that it was an Awkward Duck game, the same company that made the *Empires of Kush* series. If he recalled correctly, Awkward Duck was a subsidiary of McIntyre Simulations: Taryn's company. Since he had nothing planned for that evening, he decided to give the game a try. As he stood at the register, he couldn't help but wonder if Simulacrum had this game too, or was planning to get it. He found himself thinking of her more and more and despite his wariness, he debated on whether or not to arrange a face-to-face meeting if she was indeed in the area.

Twilight faded into night as Dominic fought to escape a hidden patch of quicksand in *Chieftain's Rise*. He'd just managed to escape, and gained a vine rope as a reward, when his cell phone rang. He peeked at the display with irritation, which was quickly replaced with a smile. He answered after putting it on speakerphone. "What's up, Twin?"

"Why are you at home on a Saturday night?" Nicollette Bastille inquired.

"Can't I just have some 'me' time?"

"Okay, the phrase 'me time' should never come out of a man's mouth," Nicollette laughed.

"Whatever. How's San Diego?"

"San Diego is San Diego."

"You sound underwhelmed."

"Eh. It is what it is."

Dominic frowned. He didn't like the tone in Nicollette's voice. "Everything alright?"

"I'm good, job's good. Matter of fact, my article on prenatal diagnosis using karyotyping just got accepted into the *Journal of Maternal-Fetal Medicine*, and I've been invited to speak on the topic at an upcoming conference in Ireland."

"Congratulations! Why don't you sound more excited?"

Nicollette brushed off his concern. "I am excited, but I've been in surgery for the past eight hours and breakfast is a distant memory. But enough about me. What's up with you?"

Dominic knew his twin well enough to know that she would talk about what was bothering her when she was good and ready, and not a minute before. He accepted the change in subject. "Playing a new game that I got this afternoon."

"You know, Mom seems to think that you've grown out of your geek stage."

Dominic jiggled his handset controls and cursed as his warrior character accidentally hit a large hive of wasps with his staff. "What she doesn't know won't hurt her." He cursed again when his character died from an overload of venomous stings and ended the level. "Dammit, I'm dead."

"Aww, poor baby. Now what is this game about?"

Dominic told her, then added, "I have to check with one of my gaming buddies to see if she got the game too."

"She? Gaming buddy?"

"The gaming community has a very significant female presence, both in front of and behind the joysticks."

"Uh huh. I'm more interested in your tone of voice when you mention your gaming buddy."

Dominic cursed to himself. His twin was extremely perceptive when it came to him. "What tone?"

"Don't play dumb, Nicky, least of all with me."

"What? We play some games together. She's a good gaming partner, and she has a good sense of humor."

And you would know this, how?"

"We private message during the games."

"Really." Nicollette's tone turned sardonic. "And how often do you play each other, or with each other, or whatever?"

Dominic shrugged. "A few times a week."

"And this has been going on for how long?"

"A few months."

"Hmm." A pause, then Nicollette asked, "Where does she live?"

"I'm not sure. Her profile indicates she may live in the Atlanta area, but I'd have to ask her."

"And if she does happen to live nearby, are you going to meet her in person?"

Dominic tried for nonchalance. "The thought had crossed my mind."

"Hmm. Well, be careful; you know the internet, in any form, is filled with the unmedicated. But it would be pretty cool if you found true love through a video game."

"Let's not jump the gun, Nicki. If I went there, I'd probably start with a phone call first."

"I wonder what what she looks like?" Nicollette mused aloud. "She's a geek too, but is she a stereotypical geek with thick glasses and zero social skills? Or is she one of those socially acceptable geeks like Neil DeGrasse Tyson?"

"I'll be sure to let you know."

"You'd have someone to watch your *Star Wars* and *Lord of the Rings* marathons with you. That's got to be worth trying to meet her. Although, you do realize that you may be engaging in an online love affair with a twelve-year-old boy in Indonesia?"

"Shut up," Dominic laughed.

"I would say that y'all would get together and have a bunch of geek babies with exceptional hand-eye coordination and the Bastille widow's peak, but we know that ain't happening."

"Not unless the Immaculate Conception strikes twice." Nicollette was the only person, other than Mark, who knew that Dominic had opted for a vasectomy three years ago.

"Seriously, the overeducated, upwardly mobile babes you've dissed and dismissed over the years don't seem to be doing it for you. Maybe it's time to test other waters. You know the definition of insanity."

"Doing the same stuff and expecting different results. True that, Twin." He stretched and yawned. "We'll see what happens. I may just continue the online fantasy; reality has a tendency to be disappointing. And what if she's ugly?"

Nicollette snorted. "You are such a Neanderthal."

"Don't hate on the Y chromosome, kid."

"Anyway." Nicollette ignored the last comment. "Let me know what happens. And if you do end up meeting Miss Dungeons and Dragons, let me know the particulars so that I can get your picture on the side of a milk carton in a timely fashion, if need be."

"Ha ha."

"I gotta bounce. I have to get back to the hospital."

"Alright. Love you."

"Love you back. Bye."

After the call disconnected, Dominic got back to the game. It had been a long time since he'd gotten killed during the first level of a game, and he had to redeem himself. He also made a mental note to get back on *Empires of Kush: Napata* and send Simulacrum a message. Maybe Nicollette was right; maybe he needed to broaden his dating horizons.

~~~

Sunday evening found Dominic cheering on that night's second-round NCAA men's basketball games at Mark's house, along with about twenty other people. Dominic and Mark were especially hyped because their undergraduate alma mater, Harvard University, had squeaked into the second round on a hot wing and a prayer to face the Florida State Seminoles.

Dominic took advantage of a commercial break to escape the two women who'd had him hemmed in on the loveseat. They'd feigned ignorance about basketball and kept peppering him with questions throughout the game, much to his annoyance. After a quick stop in the bathroom, Dominic went into the kitchen to load up on more food--and try to figure out where he could sit far away from his self-appointed bookends.

He reached for a paper plate at the same time as the short woman in front of him. A frisson of electricity flowed through his hand; when she turned her big, dark brown eyes upon him, the frisson traveled straight to the pit of his stomach. "Well, hello, Ms. McIntyre," he said with a grin.

"Dr. Bastille," Taryn greeted. The red jewels in the silver, double barbell earring in her left eyebrow winked with her surprised expression.

"I definitely didn't expect to see you here. I thought Mark said you'd moved?"

"I did, but I get back for one of Mark and Charlotte's get-togethers every now and again. I usually try to make their basketball events."

"Hoops fan?"

"No doubt. College more than pro, but it's all good. I've even been known to watch some D-League games on YouTube."

Dominic made a sweeping gesture at the stack of plates. "After you."

"Thank you." She got her plate and started to fill

it.

Dominic looked more closely at Taryn, taking in her full lips and curvaceous frame in nice-fitting jeans and tie-dyed clogs with wooden soles. Her shoulder-length, blonde-tipped dreadlocks were tied back with a burgundy-and-gold scarf that matched her Florida State T-shirt, which she'd layered over a long-sleeved, gold T-shirt. She was better looking than when they'd met during the meeting for his research project, and that was saying something. He still had fond memories of Taryn's fitted pants suit that hugged her in all the right places.

Taryn used the filling of her plate to peer at Dominic's very handsome face through her peripheral vision. He'd opted for tortoiseshell frame glasses this time, which failed to hide the devilish sparkle in his hazel eyes. His dark red fitted baseball cap, worn backwards, hid most of his prominent widow's peak.

"Well, I'd better reclaim my seat. Halftime's almost over." Taryn nodded a goodbye, finished getting her food and drink, and went back to the living room. Just as she settled into her seat on a large floor pillow in front of the couch, Dominic plopped down beside her with his own plate of food and a beer. Taryn couldn't help but notice how well his jeans molded his muscular thighs, and how his long-sleeved crimson T-shirt molded across a nice upper torso and toned biceps. She took a sip of her wine, in the hopes that it would calm her libido, which decided to make an appearance.

"Your office is in Norcross. Do you live there too?" Dominic asked as he picked up a chicken wing and gnawed on it.

Taryn nodded since her mouth was full of pizza. "Yep," she replied after she swallowed.

"Whereabouts?"

"Right off Jimmy Carter Boulevard, near the Target."

"I know where that is. One of our frat brothers lives over that way, in a gated community of townhouses." Dominic paused in his commentary while they watched Harvard go on a 10-2 run against Florida State. At the next commercial break, Dominic continued his questions. "You've developed video games too, right?"

Taryn gave him a sidelong glance. "Have you been checking up on me, Dr. Bastille?"

"It's Dominic, remember? And I can Google like anyone else. Plus, both Vincent and your company website mentioned that McIntyre Simulations started out with video games, and still does some of them."

"We do." Taryn nodded in agreement. "In fact, one of my first games still has a cult following, and still has modest sales. Have you ever heard of *Empires of Kush*?"

Dominic gave a sheepish grin, "I love that game! I play *Meroë* sometimes, but my favorite is *Napata*."

Taryn saluted him with her cup. "You are a fan. Like I said, it has a cult following. It's not as popular as, say, *Temple Treasures*."

"I don't play many of the popular games, unless you count *Assassin's Creed*, *Black Ops*, and *Madden*."

"Kinda bloodthirsty, aintcha?" Taryn cast a mock askance glance at him as she scooted an inch away from him.

"Believe it or not, it relaxes me." He shrugged. "I guess blood and guts don't bother me, since I see it every day. Or I used to." He balled up his dirty napkin and tossed it atop the denuded chicken bones on his plate. "So, what's your handle on *Empires of Kush*? You may be in our group."

"What's your group?"

"The Alchemists of Kush."

"That's my group!" Taryn's eyes sparkled with interest. "I'm Simulacrum."

Dominic froze with a potato chip halfway to his lips. "Did you just say 'Simulacrum'?"

"Yeah." Taryn looked at him strangely. "It means image, or representation. Why?"

"I know what it means." Dominic stared, then started to chuckle, which evolved into a full-blown belly laugh. Taryn noticed the two women sitting on a nearby couch; they looked at Dominic with starstruck expressions, which turned to puzzlement when their gazes passed over her. "What's so funny?"

Dominic's laugh died back down to a chuckle. "Hello, wife. Did you sew the raiment for our regiment yet?"

Taryn's mouth dropped open. "Nib-mur-re?"

"At your service, my queen." Dominic gave a seated half-bow.

No. No no no no NO. This was not good. Not only was Taryn *not* trying to mix business with pleasure--been there, done that, had the T-shirt and the soundtrack--but Dominic was indeed a fine specimen of male: the kind of fine that would get her shot, stabbed, or rooted. And she'd had her nose opened enough in her lifetime to want to avoid a repeat. She gave a weak smile and glued her eyes to the 50" flatscreen television.

Dominic noticed the sudden stiffness of Taryn's posture and tried to read her behavior. Did he go too far and offend her? Should he have kept his gaming identity private? Or, should he have not addressed her as he did in their private messages? The slight set of her jaw indicated that he may have overstepped his bounds. He had no real idea what had just gone wrong, but he was going to try and steer this conversational boat into smoother waters. "So you're a Seminoles fan?"

"Yep. My dad went there."

"Are you originally from Florida?"

"Jacksonville. You?"

"Louisiana."

Taryn eyed him again. He looked like he could be an extra in *The Feast of All Saints.* "New Orleans?" She pronounced it "N'Awlins".

"Yep, and thank you for pronouncing it correctly."

Taryn chuckled, and she relaxed slightly. "Oh, so you're one of those."

Dominic popped the last of a stuffed mushroom in his mouth. "Like most natives, it grates a bit to constantly hear the name maligned by tourists."

"So does that mean you're a Saints fan too?"

"You obviously have never met my family. Every child gets a stuffed Saints football at birth, male or female. We hemorrhage black and gold, though I did root for the Baltimore Ravens in the last Super Bowl."

"Oh, I know all about your family's obsession with the Saints." At Dominic's inquiring gaze she added, "Your sister Sheridan was not well loved during football season."

"You know Sheridan?" Dominic's grin turned sickly. Great. As much as he tried to keep his elder sister on the fringes of his life, she always managed to gain a toehold somehow.

"She was my college roommate for three years, as well as my line sister."

"Ah. So you're a Spelman girl too?"

"Yes, indeed. So you can imagine the drama Sheridan caused in Atlanta Falcons country."

"I wouldn't put it past her." Stirring the pot was one of his sister's dubious talents, as he well knew.

Thankfully, the game score became close and most conversation ceased as everyone paid close attention. It took some effort for Dominic to keep his focus on the score; Taryn's proximity was short-circuiting his brain. He thought about his twin's suggestion to go outside his romantic comfort zone, which was similar to Mark's advice a few weeks ago. He cast a sidelong glance at Taryn's locs and eyebrow ring; yep, definitely different than the women he usually dated. Maybe he was being too hasty at swearing off women. Because he'd had a streak of bad dating luck, that meant his luck was ready to change, right?

Taryn was acutely aware of Dominic's nearness,

even as she cheered on her beloved Florida State after defeating Harvard by twelve points to advance to the next round. Taryn did a happy, seated dance at her father's alma mater's victory.

Dominic watched her with an amused grin. "Now, is that any way for a *kandare* to behave?" he teased. He tried not to focus on the sensuous wiggle of Taryn's hips.

Taryn paused in her dance. "I could say the same about you, Your Highness, being a Harvard fan and all."

"I spent enough of their scholarship money during undergrad, so I should be."

"Good point." She started dancing in her seat again while humming the Florida State fight song.

"Whatever," Dominic laughed. He shifted to hide the sudden tightness in his crotch, after a quick glance to make sure his untucked shirt provided adequate coverage. Taryn's celebratory gyrations were putting all sorts of wicked thoughts into both heads. He shifted his empty plate to be on the safe side. "You guys have a really good team this year, and the Crimson were lucky to get this far."

"Well, my bracket thanks the Crimson." She brandished her cell phone, which displayed her bracket predictions in an app. "Right now, I'm ranked third in my group."

"I'm tenth in one group, fourth in another group, and somewhere near the bottom in a third group."

Taryn rose to take her empty plate into the kitchen. She shot Dominic a curious glance. "Just how many tournament groups do you belong to?"

Dominic smiled, flashing teeth that were an orthodontist's wet dream. He followed Taryn into the kitchen, admiring the fit of her jeans across her firmly rounded behind. "Three: one with some of my frat brothers, one with some other doctors, and one with some fellow Harvard alumni."

They both tossed their plates and cups into a nearby garbage can. They stared at each other for a few seconds, feeling the electricity build. Taryn broke the stare first.

"Uh, excuse me." She left the kitchen and turned in the direction of the restroom. Dominic walked over to where Mark was wrapping leftovers. "Yo, Frat, what's up with Taryn?"

Mark glanced at Dominic briefly as he finished wrapping a platter of cold cuts. "I thought you said your first meeting went well."

"It did. This is a personal inquiry."

"I thought you were swearing off women?"

"I can still inquire while trying to get my love life

in order."

"Hmm." Mark placed a foil-covered platter on an adjacent counter. "Well, since you're trying to reform and all, I'll answer your questions to the best of my ability."

"Well, for starters, is she single?"

"As far as I know," Mark replied. He turned to look at Dominic. "You do know that she lives in Norcross, right?"

"I know. I'll have to go to her office at some point to view the simulations for my research project." Dominic shrugged. "So?"

"So, long distance ain't exactly your thing. And you always make it a point never to mix business with pleasure. You don't even date anyone who works at the same hospital as you."

"Norcross is only twenty, thirty minutes away. Nell lived in Sandy Springs, which is farther than that. And not dating in the workplace is the best way to avoid a sexual harassment suit, or other relationship-oriented drama."

"Says the man whose ex-fiancée is now just an interoffice phone call away." Mark tore off a piece of foil and grinned as Dominic flipped his middle finger. "As for the distance thing, I stand corrected. But in my defense, you usually get bored if a woman lives more than ten minutes away."

"I'm getting into quality over quantity; or rather, premium over proximity."

"Uh huh. Well, Taryn's got it covered on both of those ends, but you need to make sure that you can give her what she deserves." He stared at Dominic, all joking aside. "I'm serious, Dominic. If you're going to keep running a roster, leave Taryn alone. That's not her flow."

"Sometimes you have to step outside your comfort zone to get what you want." Dominic looked in the direction of the living room. "It's worth a try."

Mark shook his head. "You are killing me with the turning over of a new leaf. We need to draft you a player, quick."

"Whatever."

~~~

When Taryn exited the restroom she was waylaid by Charlotte, who hailed her from a guest bedroom. She was sorting the guests' coats and jackets that had been stored on the bed.

"Did you have a good time?" Charlotte asked as she dug through the pile and handed Taryn her coat. Charlotte was also a member of the same sorority as Taryn, but gained membership through a graduate chapter in a different state.

"I did, thank you. Especially since Florida State won."

"I'll bet." Charlotte picked up a tartan plaid wool muffler. "I noticed you having a good conversation with Dominic."

"Yeah. I'm actually doing some work for him, on a research project."

"I heard; Mark told me about it the other day. Congratulations." She folded a leather trench coat in two and laid it on the bed. "Maybe you can help take his mind off things."

"Uh, how?" Taryn was confused. "I'm just working on his sims. I won't even see him most of the time; I'll be in my own lab, in Norcross."

"You may see him more than you think; he loves his research almost as much as he loves surgery." Charlotte exhaled and put her hands on her hips. "He won't admit it, but his promotion is taking its toll. He has a lot more going on these days." Charlotte folded the plaid muffler and laid it atop the leather trench coat. The soft light from the bedside lamp danced over the burgundy highlights in her black, chin-length bob. "You two seemed interested in a lot more than basketball out there."

Taryn laughed. "You're seeing things, Chuck. We

were just discussing the game."

"Mmhmm. Well, just be careful. Dominic is actually rather sweet, and he's a brilliant, gifted surgeon, but he has a well-deserved reputation with the ladies. I don't want you to end up a statistic."

"I saw firsthand his effect on the female persuasion during the meeting at his job, so don't worry. There's nothing to be careful about." She slid into her knee-length wool coat. "Well, let me roll out. I have a lot to do tomorrow."

"Another project?"

"Of course. But this one is more personal, and I haven't had much time to work on it."

Charlotte accompanied Taryn back to the kitchen, where she said goodbye to Mark. Dominic was still in the kitchen, chatting with Mark as he continued to put away leftovers. He looked at Taryn as she entered.

"You guys need some help straightening up?" Taryn asked between people stopping in to say their goodnights and thank yous.

"We're good, T," Mark replied as he dumped the few remaining wilted leaves of a tossed salad in the garbage. "Our cleaning lady comes in tomorrow morning."

"Cleaning lady? My, my, we sho' have arrived,"

Taryn teased.

Charlotte gestured around the kitchen. "As you can see, the way my husband leaves the kitchen after making one of his signature creations, you'd hire one too."

"Hey!" Mark protested as everyone laughed.

"Alright then." She and Charlotte exchanged hugs. "I'll call you tomorrow."

"Cool, maybe we can grab lunch this week. Hey, how are you getting back home?" Charlotte asked with a frown.

"Same way I got here: I drove."

"That's right; you finally broke down and bought a car."

"Last month. I didn't have much of a choice. You know MARTA doesn't go out that far, and Gwinnett County Transit is sparse in my area. Plus, a lot of my clients are inside the Perimeter."

Mark closed the refrigerator door after depositing two zip-locked bags of cold cuts. "What kind of car did you get?"

"A Tesla Model S."

"Whoa." Mark was impressed. "Isn't that the electric car that can drive itself? I read about it in *PC Magazine*."

"It has limited auto-drive capabilities, but yes, that's the one."

"Do you ever use anything that isn't computer-operated?" Charlotte laughed.

"Not if I can help it," Taryn grinned.

Dominic had been following their conversation and saw an opening. "Where did you park?" he asked Taryn.

"A couple of blocks down."

"I'm about to leave myself, and I'm going that way. I'll walk you to your car." He ignored Mark's barely concealed smirk and Charlotte's amused eye roll.

Charlotte saw Taryn open her mouth to protest and quickly cut her off. "Even though this neighborhood is fairly safe, you still don't need to be walking around outside, at night, by yourself."

"I did it all the time when I lived in Cali," Taryn protested. "And I have pepper spray."

"You're not in Cali, and pepper spray only works if you're able to get it out of your pocket in time to use it." She shot Taryn a "no arguments" look before she switched her gaze to Dominic. "It's settled, then. Thanks, Dominic. I appreciate it."

Taryn bit back her retort. "Thank you then, Dominic."

"No problem." He kissed Charlotte on the cheek and exchanged coded handshakes with Mark. "Charlotte, thanks for having me over. Mark, I'll catch up with you later." Dominic grabbed his jacket and pulled his keys out of his pocket. "Ready?"

Taryn nodded and followed him downstairs and out of the house. They walked down the quiet, tree-lined street. Soon, they stopped in front of a silver sedan. "This is me," Taryn said.

Dominic eyed the Tesla and whistled low. "I've read about Teslas, but I've never seen one up close. It looks like a sweet ride."

"It gets the job done."

"Good mileage? I mean, it's electric, right?"

"Right. Pretty good mileage. It's not a road trip kind of car, though."

"How do you charge it?"

"I have a charger in my garage, and another at my work."

Dominic walked around the car, admiring its sleek lines. "You mentioned that you recently bought it. Any buyer's remorse? Do you miss a regular, gas-fueled car?"

"No, and no. It's comfortable, I don't have to worry about gas fuel, and I love the auto-pilot feature."

She pressed a button on her key fob. The rear and headlights flashed, as the alarm was disengaged with a chirp. The engine purred to life with a low rumble.

Dominic tried to stall for time, so he could talk to her more. "Where did you get it? Is there a Tesla dealership around here?"

"Out by Lenox Square Mall." She opened the driver's side door and slid into the bucket seat. "Thanks for the escort."

"Again, no problem." He fidgeted, then said, "I'd ask if you wanted a nightcap, but there's not much open around here at this time of night on a Sunday.".

"Thanks, but I have lot to do tomorrow. "

Dominic nodded. "Understood. Raincheck?"

"Are you asking me on a date, Nib-mur-re?"

"Yes."

Taryn tilted her head and looked up at him. Dominic was definitely easy on the eyes, and had the kind of swagger that held her attention. But he probably had binders full of women on tap. And there was the small matter of her working on his research project, which had the capacity to take McIntyre Simulations to another level, with a whole source of untapped clientele. "We'll see."

"Well, let me know if you change your mind.

Otherwise, I'll see you online."

Taryn nodded and got in  her car. Dominic shut the door behind her.

"Make sure you wear your seatbelt. See you around." Dominic winked and walked half a block down to where his own car was parked. Taryn watched until he got in his car, then pulled off and headed home.

## 5.

The ring of Taryn's cell phone interrupted her writing flow. She looked at the Caller ID screen with some irritation, which gave way to curiosity. "Dr. Bastille."

"Taryn," Dominic greeted her. "Just calling to see if you have any updates?"

It had only been a week, but Taryn was used to dealing with antsy clients who expected technology to deliver results five minutes ago--even for more complex projects such as simulations. "I have, though it may not be as far along as you'd like."

"I apologize; I know it's only been a week and you said two weeks. It's not like you're doing something simple, but..." he sighed. "I'm just really excited about the possibilities that could advance medicine as we know it.

And, I have a lot of grant money riding on this."

"I'll live. Plus, Cecily Porter has already called."

"She did?"

"Earlier this morning."

Dominic frowned. Cecily had no right questioning Taryn about his research. "What did you tell her?"

"That I was sure that you would pass on any pertinent information to her as the project progresses."

Dominic chuckled. He was sure that went over as well as Louis Farrakhan at a Ku Klux Klan rally.

Taryn looked at the calendar on her computer. "Did you want to come up and see what I have already?"

"Today?"

"Not necessarily, but when you can spare a moment."

Dominic checked his own calendar for the rest of the day: meetings, meetings, and more meetings. "Uh...would this afternoon be too soon?"

"I can be available after three. You may get caught up in traffic, though."

"How about three-thirty?"

"That's fine."

"Cool. See you then. "

Taryn went back to her programming, during which she went back and forth between some articles she'd found on the internet about Dominic, and something called ex-vivo graft technique. The technique basically involved the repair of less-than-perfect organs outside of the body, in order to make them available for transplant. This technique was done occasionally but according to the articles, Atlanta Transplant Consortium transplanted a rather significant amount of repaired organs. And Dominic Bastille was one of the region's experts on this ex-vivo technique. She wanted to incorporate this technique into her sims, but she needed to figure out exactly how it was done. Dominic's visit was coming at a very good time.

Taryn tapped her fingers on her keyboard thoughtfully. So Dominic Bastille had a brain and some skills to back up that pretty face. Brains and beauty: always a dangerous combination.

~~~

At 2:30, Dominic shut down his computer and tossed his lab coat over the back of his chair. He'd just turned off the lamp on his desk when Cecily walked in.

"Leaving early? That's a first," she commented as she stood in the doorway. At his frown, she added, "And before you ask, Lori isn't at her desk right now."

"I'm headed to McIntyre Simulations to check on the progress that Taryn's made." He grabbed his tablet from his desk.

"You can't do that over the phone? Rush hour traffic has already started."

"She said during the meeting that she'd need me to come to her office lab and actually see the sims; it's not like she can bring them here." He removed his keys from his pocket and strode toward the door.

"Well, I'll ride with you. Just wait a few minutes while I go and grab my purse."

Dominic raised an eyebrow. "I can handle it from here, Cecily, thanks. I'm sure you have more pressing matters to attend to."

"But I thought she hadn't finished the mock sim yet?"

"Yeah, about that." Dominic paused and turned back to Cecily. "I don't appreciate you checking up on my project without my permission. Taryn deals with me, and me only."

Cecily pressed her lips into a thin line and smoothed her hands down the front of her fitted, lime green suit. "Dominic, it's my job to make sure that this project goes smoothly and reflects positively upon ATC."

"No, it's your job to make sure that whatever I do is spun positively to the public. It's my job to make sure the project goes smoothly. And I have a better idea of how to do that than you do. If there's something you need to know about the project, I'll let you know."

Cecily stiffened. "If you don't want me to come along, then just say so."

"I don't want you to come along." Dominic moved to walk past her, where she was still blocking the doorway. "Excuse me."

Cecily's nostrils flared and she stepped aside. She watched Dominic walk down the hall toward the elevators with a sour look on her face. Dominic rode the elevator down to the lobby and walked over to the employee area of the adjacent garage. As he pulled out into the notorious Atlanta traffic, he shook his head at Cecily's audacity. He'd hoped that working for the same place would require them to be civil and professional, but she obviously had a problem with blurring the professional and personal. Eventually, one of them would have to leave ATC and he knew that it wouldn't be him. But Cecily was good at her job, and the publicity from his research--if he could get it at the level that he envisioned--would bring in even more research grants and really put ATC on the map. Still, Dominic wondered how long he'd have to put up with Cecily's attempts to insinuate herself back into his life. Had he known she'd be joining ATC's staff, he would have asked for more money.

Dominic plugged the address of McIntyre Simulations into his car's GPS and followed the directions. Traffic wasn't as bad as he'd anticipated, and he arrived ten minutes early. He looked the nondescript building façade and walked to the main entrance, where a placard with red and gold letters professed it to be the home of McIntyre Simulations. He exited the car and looked around at the parking lot dotted with cars; there was nothing in the office park but one- and two-story buildings made of brick and/or concrete, with treated windows looking out onto the parking lots adjacent to each building. Trees lined the perimeter that was further delineated by neatly cut grass. He spotted Taryn's silver Tesla parked in the shade of a small group of trees, with one of those accordion-folded sun shields in the windshield.

As Dominic approached the door, he heard a loud click, followed by a long buzz. He hesitated, then pulled open the door. He removed his sunglasses as he stood in the lobby and looked around, not that there was much to see. There was no receptionist or any other human, or seating area for visitors; just a long table with literature on the company, and an elevator. He looked around for a telephone, or intercom, or some way of contacting someone and alerting them to his arrival. He'd just pulled his phone out of his pocket to call Taryn when the elevator doors opened and she walked out. "Hey," he said as relief crept into his voice. "I was about to call you and let you know I was here."

"I already knew you were here." Taryn pointed to the discreet video cameras nestled in the decorative molding atop the walls, and to small, waist-height gray boxes that blended into the walls. "The motion detectors notified me that someone was in the lobby, and I looked on the video feed to see that it was you." She held up her wrist to indicate her smartwatch. "Plus, I knew you were coming, so I've been keeping an eye out." And Dominic certainly provided a lovely eyeful, in black wool dress slacks, glossy black leather loafers, and a V-neck hunter green cashmere sweater that brought out the green flecks in his hazel eyes.

"I see." Dominic tried not to feel as if he was falling down the rabbit hole. He considered himself rather tech-savvy, but Taryn's world was on a different level.

Taryn gestured toward the elevator. "Ready?"

"Lead the way." Dominic noticed that Taryn was dressed down today, much as she'd been at Mark and Charlotte's house. Well-fitting jeans that accentuated curves in all the right places, partially covered by an oversized green shirt that was layered over what looked like a beige tank top. Green and gold sneakers were on her feet, and her locs swung freely about her shoulders. The gold tips were an unintentional accent of her shoes. Taryn held her smartwatch up to a small black square on the elevator panel and pushed the "Up" button.

They rode for a few seconds until the door opened on a floor that was the opposite of the stillness in the lobby. People in various stages of casual dress stood in the open workspace, either at waist-high podiums or counters that ran around the edges of the room. Glassed-in offices were behind the counters, and some contained more people who sat at desks topped with multiple computer monitors and spoke into headsets. The atmosphere, which was at rather chilly internal temperature, was abuzz with tech chatter. Some also carried or drank from various beverages--Dominic noted they tended to run to either caffeinated soft drinks or coffee--as the tapped away at computer keyboards, or jabbed and gestured at monitors.

Taryn led Dominic through the maze of hyped-up tech bodies until they reached a long hallway. A large, glassed-in office sparkled in the afternoon sunlight, courtesy of the large window that took up a significant part of one wall.

"My office," Taryn said as she gestured toward a comfortably padded chair. "Have a seat. Want some water, or something?"

"Water would be great, thanks."

Taryn reached into a waist-high refrigerator near her wooden desk and removed a bottle of water, which she handed to Dominic. Their fingers touched, and Taryn felt a frisson of electricity not unlike the one she'd experienced when she accidentally touched Dominic's hand at Mark and Charlotte's. She quickly pulled her hand away and shut the office door, bringing a welcome wash of silence to Dominic's ears. Taryn settled into her large, high-backed office chair. She turned the large monitor nearest Dominic so that he could see it as well.

"Okay, this is what I've come up with so far." She tapped a sequence of buttons and the MacSim logo popped up, along with the project number and Taryn's name as the lead developer. "This is a standard medical sim, which I customized based on your transplant needs. As I said over the phone, it's only been a week, so there is a lot of room for improvement and input." She tapped another key sequence and a simulation of a man appeared: white male, approximately thirty years of age, short brown hair covered with a sterile head covering, brown eyes. He lay on a gurney and was draped in sterile blue surgical cloths. The gurney was in a surgical suite. "I figured that you wanted to get to the nitty gritty, as in how to actually transplant a kidney. But if you want some pre-surgical training sims that are specific to the transplantation field, I can easily add that."

"That would be good."

"Alright." She tapped more buttons and wiggled her mouse. "Here, you can use your mouse, or finger if you're on a touch screen, to move the scalpel over the patient's abdomen. I've also included gauges where you can monitor blood pressure, heart rate, and the time left on anesthesia." She clicked the mouse to display other tools. "You can then use the mouse to select other surgical tools, like forceps, and use the for the transplant procedure. This particular sim is for transplanting a kidney into someone, but I can also make one for removing a kidney for transplant. Your call."

"You've done all this in a week?" Dominic shook his head in amazement. "Wow."

Taryn shrugged. "I love my work, and this is interesting."

"Well, that's a really good start."

"When I'm done, I'll email you a link to the sim so that you can try it out yourself. I'd like you to do it on both a desktop and a tablet, if you don't mind. I assume you want it functional in both stationary and mobile systems?"

Dominic nodded, pleased that Taryn was hitting all of his project wants so far. "Yes. Medicine is adapting more to technology, and tablet computers--even smartphones-- are becoming even more important for everything from recordkeeping to viewing medical test results."

Taryn raised her pierced eyebrow. "I thought that was just something they did on *Grey's Anatomy*, for entertainment value."

"Some hospital systems have been slow to adopt the use of tablets and computerized medical records, but that's more about funding than anything. Still, it's where medicine is headed, so soon they won't have a choice."

Taryn nodded, and they sat in companionable silence as Dominic stared at the incomplete sim on the screen with pride. "Hey, do you want the fifty-cent tour of MacSim?"

"Cool." Dominic rose from his seat and followed Taryn out of her office.

Taryn waved a hand at the large, air-conditioned room. "This, in case you haven't noticed, is the main work area. Most of the programmers have their computers here, and do the main coding for their various assigned projects." They walked out of the large room and back to the main hallway in front of the elevators Taryn turned right and pointed to a sizeable room outfitted with long tables and bench-style seating. "This is the break room. Programmers work all hours, so there's usually someone in here all the time."

"You're open twenty-four/seven?" Dominic asked in surprise as he noted the two large stainless steel refrigerators and vending machines for soft drinks and energy drinks. Three Keurig coffee makers, as well as an espresso machine, took up counter space next to a hot plate and a toaster oven; all of these appliances were bookended by two microwaves. A water cooler stood in a corner.

Taryn nodded. "It's either that or allow them to take corporate property home to work on, and that's not allowed except for my upper management. Plus, business has been good for the past year, so the extra work time helps us get projects out on time." They left the break room and continued down the hall, where Taryn pointed out smaller rooms with fewer computers. "This is where people go to work on the next phase of their projects, like what I've done so far on your sims." She pointed through the large glass window to the glossy white wall at the far end of the room. A programmer was playing an educational sim on the large screen. "Sims can be projected onto that screen and played with game consoles, like you would with a PS4 or Xbox. This is where we get most of the kinks out."

They walked down to a smaller, dogleg hallway, which led to a large white door. A darkened palm plate and a smaller black square right above it rested near the doorjamb. "We do the final phases on more sensitive projects in there." She gestured at the door as they walked by.

On their way back to Taryn's office, she asked, "I have a question. I looked up the ex-vivo technique online. You're one of the leading experts in ex-vivo graft implementation, and the Atlanta Transplant Consortium is unique in that in that it transplants a significant number of organs that have been repaired ex-vivo. Has this had any effect on your mortality rates?"

Dominic shook his head as they reentered her office and took their respective seats. "No. Our mortality rates fall within, if not lower, than the national average. This is because with the use of repaired organs, there is an increase in the number of patients who receive transplants, which in turn decreases the mortality rates due to pre-transplant-related deaths. "

"The ex-vivo technique basically means that you are repairing any minor damage to certain organs outside of the body, in sterile conditions, so that they may be acceptable for transplant. How do you combat the stigma that you are an organ thrift shop, or that you are relegating organs to the level of a pre-owned car?"

Dominic blinked. "An organ thrift shop and pre-owned cars. Wow." He bit back a laugh at the analogies. "While organs repaired by the ex-vivo technique may not be as aesthetically pleasing as organs procured directly from a donor in a more traditional way, I assure you that ex-vivo organs are completely functional. We have been vetted by the Surgeon General of the United States, the United Organ Sharing Network, The Organ Procurement and Transplantation Network, the Food & Drug Administration...you name the regulatory body, and they have signed off on the organs we transplant."

"But ex-vivo is normally used on livers; yet, you have expanded this practice to include kidneys and livers."

"You have done your homework." Dominic nodded, impressed. "That is correct."

"How is it that you are able to do this? Aren't kidneys and livers more vulnerable?"

"They are, but that's a large part of my research.

There is too large a demand for kidneys and not enough supply. Ex vivo increases the amount of organs available for transplant, which makes for shorter wait times on the UNOS list."

"So how are you able to repair kidneys and livers, if they are so delicate?"

"I created the technique that combines microsurgery with biochemical alterations that not only allow for the ex-vivo repair of friable organ tissue, but also reduces the rate of organ rejection in post-transplantation patients."

"The Bastille Technique is only done here?"

Dominic chuckled. His grandfather was probably turning in his grave at the moniker Taryn granted. "The Bastille Technique was my late grandfather's suturing technique."

"Then what is yours called?"

"The Bastille Technique," Dominic admitted. They exchanged a laugh. "I guess, having grown up around Lucien Bastille, I always associate that name with him. But I guess my ex vivo technique does qualify for its own name."

"It's easier to remember," Taryn teased.

"Whatever," Dominic laughed again. "But back to your question. Unless there's another Bastille doing it, yes, the new Bastille Technique is only done at the ATC, and ATC is the only facility in the Northern Hemisphere doing ex-vivo repair and transplantation on this scale. And while I have many talented siblings and cousins who are physicians, they are not me." His smile was nothing short of smug.

Taryn refrained from rolling her eyes. He had more nerve than a toothache and an overabundance of charm, which only stoked flutter in her lower belly. She pressed her knees together and asked another question. "What made you go into the organ transplantation field?"

"Transplantation is like a jigsaw puzzle to me, and I love jigsaw puzzles. I like finding that one piece of the jigsaw that can help someone live a longer life."

Taryn nodded. "Looks like  you inherited your grandfather's surgical skill."

"Perhaps."

Taryn was surprised at the sudden coolness of his tone. "How do you think he'd feel about your progress as a surgeon?"

Dominic shrugged. "Excellence is expected of a Bastille."

The frostiness of his voice made Taryn wish she'd worn a sweater. She started to ask another question when her watch started to flash. She tapped the face and looked at it, then switched to one of the computers on her desk and toggled the mouse. "I didn't know Cecily was coming today. I would have held off on the tour until she arrived."

Dominic looked confused. "She wasn't."

"Well, she's here."

"Here where?"

"Downstairs in the lobby. Someone must have buzzed her in." She gestured to the screen, which showed the views of some of the the security cameras posted around the company. This particular set included the ones in the lobby, which showed Cecily standing impatiently in front of the elevators as she pressed the "up" button in vain.

Dominic's expression darkened. "She wasn't supposed to come. I told her specifically that any and all project discussions were between you and me, and that I would apprise her of any information when necessary." He gave Taryn a pointed look.

Taryn shrugged. "I don't talk to anyone but my clients about their projects, and you are my client, not Atlanta Transplant Consortium. We take confidentiality seriously around here." She gestured again to the computer screen. "How do you want to handle this?"

"I've got it." Dominic stood, his hardened

expression eliciting a brief twinge of sympathy from Taryn, for Cecily. "Please call me when you've finished the mockup sims."

Taryn nodded as she escorted him back downstairs to the lobby. When they exited the elevator, Cecily was surprised to see Dominic leaving, and that Taryn was with him.

"Oh, hi, Dominic. I was hoping to catch you before you'd left here." Her bright smile held a tinge of nervousness around the edges. "I wanted to see Taryn's setup, maybe get some pictures for next month's ATC newsletter."

"I'm done here. You wasted gas." Dominic pushed past her and out the door.

Cecily's smile died at the controlled fury in Dominic's voice. She watched him leave, then turned back to Taryn with her jaw firmed in resolve. "Any chance I could get a tour of the premises?" Cecily flashed what she hoped was a winning smile.

Taryn folded her arms across her chest. "Now's not a good time. You really should have called ahead; I could have saved you a trip."

"Right." Cecily swallowed and fiddled with the designer sunglasses in her hand. "Well, how was your meeting with Dr. Bastille?"

"Enlightening. I have a much better idea of what Dr. Bastille wants and needs."

Cecily narrowed her eyes at the possibility of unspoken context in that sentence. She pursed her lips and slid on her sunglasses. "I see. Well, you have a good evening." She turned on her high heels and sashayed out of the door. Taryn shook her head and went back upstairs to her office.

Her watch gave two long buzzes, indicating an incoming call. She checked the Caller ID: it was Dominic. She pressed the screen to activate the Bluetooth headphones around her neck. "Taryn McIntyre."

"What are you doing for dinner tonight?" Dominic asked without preamble.

Strains of music wafted through the headset, and Taryn figured that Dominic must be in his car. "Probably whipping something up at home. Why?"

"There's a really good steak place near here, if you like steak. Ever been to Stoney River?"

"Of course. And what do you mean, 'near here'? Where are you?"

"Sitting in your parking lot. So, how about it?"

Taryn twisted her bottom lip as she closed the door to her office. She'd gotten burned once, mixing business with pleasure, and had the legal bills to prove it.

"I love steak, and I love Stoney River, but I don't mix business with pleasure."

"We can talk some more about my project. This would be discussing our workload, over a meal."

Taryn couldn't help but laugh at Dominic's mimic of Eddie Murphy's tone in the movie *Boomerang*, when his character Marcus invited Robin Givens's character Jacqueline over to dinner. "I don't know, Dominic..."

"When's the last time you ate?"

Taryn had a vague recollection of a Clif bar grabbed on the fly, on her way to a meeting with one of her project groups.

"See, you can't even remember and if you did eat something, it probably was something like a granola bar." Dominic had correctly interpreted both her silence and her habits. "You have to eat, right? And I'm not too keen on battling rush-hour traffic on the beltway. So you'd be doing me a solid, and getting your belly filled. Kill two birds."

Taryn looked down at her jeans and sneakers. "I'm not dressed for Stoney River. I'd need to go home to change."

"That's cool. There's a Starbucks up the street; I can kill some time there, get some work done. I'll pick you up at your house around 7, if that's not too late."

Taryn sighed. Maybe this time would be different. And she'd make sure to keep it strictly business. And she was getting hungry. "Seven is fine. I'll text you my address."

"Bet. See you at seven."

Taryn disconnected the call and stared blankly at her computer screen. *What just happened?*

~~~

Later on, at home, she was on the phone with Sheridan when she accidentally let it slip about Dominic.

"What are you up to this weekend?" Taryn asked her friend.

"Chapter meeting, then going to the soccer game of my Little Sister." Sheridan was an active participant in the Big Brothers and Sisters program. "Then, I may go out, or I may stay in and order in. What about you?"

"Don't know about the weekend, but I have a date tonight."

"With Ryan?"

"Nope. Haven't heard from him since he left for China last month, on business."

"Someone new?" Sheridan let out a cheer. "It's about time! You've been holding out, ma'am. I want all the pertinent info, stat!"

Taryn laughed, even as she tried to figure how to mention Dominic without mentioning him by name. "Not much to tell right now. I just met him a couple of weeks ago, through my work."

"And it took you this long to get a date?"

"I don't like mixing business with pleasure."

"True." Sheridan was well aware of the legal drama Taryn went through in California when she had dated a guy at her job. "So what changed your mind about this guy?"

"He's a pest. And a slick one at that. Not only did he wear me down, but he set it up in a way that kind of backed me into a corner."

"And you liked it," Sheridan snickered. "I like him already. What's his name?"

"Uh..." Taryn thought fast. "Nick." She remembered Sheridan once referring to Dominic that way, so she assumed that it was a valid nickname.

"Nick. Okay. What does he do?"

"He's a doctor."

"Ooh, what's his last name? What's his specialty? I may know him, or know someone who knows him. You know I gotta do due diligence for my homie."

Taryn realized that she had to come clean. "Bastille," she answered with a sigh and an anticipatory wince at Sheridan's possible reaction.

"Bastille?" Sheridan's tone was puzzled. "I have one cousin named Nick, but he's an architect in Nevada, and he's only twenty-five years old...hold up. Are you talking about *Dominic*? As in, my little brother Dominic?"

"Yeah."

"You're going out with my brother? How did that happen?"

Taryn recounted Dominic's invitation, complete with the Eddie Murphy *Boomerang* voice. Sheridan let loose a peal of laughter. "Shut your face!"

Taryn failed to see the humor. "What's so funny?"

"Man, you just don't know." Sheridan's laughter died down to a chuckle. "So Dominic asked you out, huh? Interesting."

"Why interesting?"

"I love my brother, pain in the ass that he is, but Dominic tends to date high-maintenance, model-looking types. You know, the ones with weekly standing hair and nail appointments, subscriptions to *Vogue*, a closet full of Jimmy Choos, and gym-sculpted bodies."

Taryn knew all too well the type of woman Sheridan described. "Like Cecily Porter?"

"Exactly like...wait. You've met Cecily?"

"Unfortunately. She's head of PR, or whatever, at

Dominic's job."

"*What?!*" Sheridan shrieked. "What the hell? Since when?"

"I don't know. I just know that she was there when I met with Dominic and the executive team of his job about his research project, and she kept popping up at the oddest of times when Dominic and I were discussing his project on the strictly business tip."

Sheridan let loose with a string of invectives that made Taryn, who had long gotten used to Sheridan's profanity, raise her eyebrows in surprise. "I take it you don't like Cecily?"

"That shady, money-grubbing, social-climbing bitch made my brother's life miserable. We popped a bottle of Champagne when their engagement was called off."

"They were engaged?"

"Yeah, about three or so years ago. Allegedly, Cecily called it off but that didn't make any sense; she'd chased Dominic down to get that ring on her finger, and I doubted she would give up so easily. Plus, it was less than a month before the wedding: invitations had been sent, caterers had finalized orders, the bridesmaids had our dresses and whatnot. I think Dominic called it quits but let her say otherwise, as a favor."

Now Cecily's behavior made a lot of sense to Taryn. But an ex-fiancée was a whole different kettle of fish than an ex-girlfriend in the hierarchy of relationships, which meant that she'd have to be extra careful with Dominic. He had feelings enough to want to marry Cecily at some point, and she was still around, so something may have still been lingering between them.

Sheridan must have sensed what was on Taryn's mind. "Don't trip about Cecily. My brother ain't trying to go back down that road, trust."

"So *you* say. But she's around him every day at work, and afterward for all I know."

"Dominic may not have had much of a choice for her to be at his work; her father is a surgeon, and has a lot of connections. It's partially how Cecily has managed to get some of her shine: her daddy has pulled some strings here and there for his baby girl. It's an open secret back home. Anyway, I wouldn't be surprised if she finagled that job through her dad, just to get next to Dominic."

"I thought you said that I shouldn't trip about her? If she did indeed hustle her dad to get her job to be around Dominic, then I'm putting myself in the crosshairs of some unstable, stalkerish behavior. I'm not trying for a repeat of sophomore year." Taryn had dated a guy at

Clark Atlanta University her sophomore year, and his on-again, off-again ex-girlfriend took offense. What had started out as a pleasant evening of Blockbuster rental movies and local takeout ended up with the kinda ex screaming outside of the guy's apartment building and trying to jimmy the lock on the outside building door with a butter knife. The guy went outside to calm her down, which led to them tussling in the street until the police came. Taryn stayed in his apartment, terrified, clutching a baseball bat that rested in the corner of the guy's living room in case the girl made her way into the apartment. Needless to say, she avoided the guy's apologetic phone calls and pleas for forgiveness until he gave up and went away. Taryn heard through mutual friends that he'd gotten back together (again) with the psycho, kinda ex.

Sheridan understood the reference. "I don't think Cecily would go that far," she reassured, though there was a bit of hesitancy in her voice."

Taryn picked up on it. "But you don't know for sure."

"No, I don't," Sheridan admitted. "I mean, I also thought that Cecily had gotten over Dominic by now; last I heard, she was back home in New Orleans. Regardless, Dominic wouldn't let anything happen to you. He'll check

Cecily, if he hasn't already."

Taryn dismissed Sheridan's faith in her brother's ability to back Cecily off him and, by extension, Taryn. She'd seen the smartest of men become stupid around certain women. "Well, since I don't seem to be his type, he probably just wants to be friends."

"Most men don't want to be 'just friends' with a woman, no matter what they say. And Dominic hasn't had a strictly female friend in I don't know how long. He usually reserves that role for Nicollette."

"Who's Nicollette?"

"His twin sister."

"That's right; you mentioned once that you had twin siblings."

"Yep. Technically, she's the baby of the family, since she was born four minutes after Dominic. She's a prettier version of him; it's kind of scary how much they look alike, even for twins. She's a pediatric surgeon on the West Coast."

"I'm starting to rethink this date thing," Taryn mused as she twisted her bottom lip in agitation. "It might be best for me to keep things strictly professional."

"Don't you back your monkey ass out now," Sheridan cackled. "It ain't gonna happen. My little brother is pig-headed and determined."

"So am I."

"Hate to break it to you, T-Mac, but you may have met your match in Dominic. Don't let the pretty fool you; he's got a big brain behind those hazel eyes. And he's relatively sane, believe it or not." Sheridan sighed. "As much as I hate to admit it, if you get past his flirtiness and womanizing ways, he's actually quite sweet. And he's loyal. He'll ride or die for you, if you've earned it."

Taryn looked at the clock on her nightstand. "Well, I'd better go get ready for my dinner date."

"I'm still amused at how Dominic just Bogarted your time. That's typical Dominic behavior, but you usually don't allow stuff like that to happen."

"Guess I'm slipping in my old age. He caught me in a weak moment, when my stomach was growling. Anyway, it's a free meal."

"He won't be taking you to McDonald's, either. I will give my brother that: he's not cheap. Did he say where you were going?"

"That steak place near my house that you and I went to, the last time you visited."

"Stoney River? That was one of the best steaks I ever had in my life. And nice atmosphere.
I approve."

"So glad you do," Taryn said drily.

"What are you wearing?"

"I don't know yet." Taryn walked over to her closet and went inside to look over her choices.

"Wear a dress. I told you, Dominic likes girly girls."

"Which again begs the question, why did he ask me out?"

"Dominic has always had a keen eye for beauty, in whatever form it takes. You should definitely take it as a compliment that you're on his radar. I have yet to see him with anyone ugly."

"You're not helping. Let me get off this phone and get ready."

"Wear something form-fitting, to show off your butt, and short enough to show your legs. Wear your locs down. And call me tomorrow with the details!"

Taryn laughed and disconnected the call while she rifled through the clothes hanging on both sides of her closet. She needed an outfit that showed she was making an effort, but not trying to be something she wasn't.

An hour later, Taryn's doorbell rang and she answered the door. Dominic stood on the other side, neatly turned out in the same outfit he'd worn earlier. "Hi." She waved him into the house.

"Hi." Dominic stepped into the foyer and bent to kiss her on the cheek. He straightened and .looked around with curiosity. There were metal and crystal light fixtures on the beige-striped walls, which gave off a soft light through the frosted glass bulb covers. He could see part of the living room to the right of the foyer, and part of the kitchen to the left. At the end of the short hallway was a set of stairs, and beyond that a door that he presumed led to the backyard. He turned his attention back to Taryn's outfit, appreciating the way the brown sweater dress hugged a nice set of curves and how her high-heeled brown leather boots set off a pair of toned, long legs. "You look great."

"Thank you. So do you." She ran a hand over her locs, which were gathered softly back from her face with a wide, patterned scarf and spilled across her shoulders. The scent of his woodsy cologne lingered. "Ready to go?"

"Sure. We have reservations at 7:30." Dominic waited for her to gather her purse, then he stepped outside while she set the house alarm by tapping her smartwatch. He escorted her to his car, which was parked in the driveway. The scent of her perfume, something deeply floral, appealed to him.

Once they were both settled in, Dominic backed

out of the driveway and headed toward Jimmy Carter Boulevard. They made small talk until they reached the restaurant. Dominic was surprised to see the hostess greet Taryn by name as she picked up two leather-bound menus and led them to their table. "You come here a lot?"

"At least once a week in person, though I pick up lunch here a couple of times a week," Taryn answered after they were seated and given their menus. "Sometimes I ask them to send dinner up to my staff if they're running hot on a project."

"So you're like a VIP here."

"Nothing like that, " Taryn laughed. "I just like supporting local businesses. And the food is good."

Their server came to take their drink orders, then left again.

"Here's to crossed paths and a spectacular research project," Dominic toasted when they had their drinks.

Taryn's lips quirked up in a smile. "To crossed paths," she echoed as she clinked the rim of her glass of red wine against Dominic's bourbon-filled highball glass. They sipped and looked around the crowded restaurant before looking back at each other.

"So, Taryn, tell me about yourself."

Taryn shrugged. "Not much to tell. You know

what I do for a living, that I went to college with your sister Sheridan, I used to live near Mark and Charlotte, and that I like college basketball. What else do you want to know?"

"Indulge me."

Taryn sipped her wine. "Well, I grew up in Jacksonville, Florida. I got a full scholarship to Spelman and graduated with a double major in mathematics and computer science, where I was recruited for a job with a defense contractor company. I moved to northern California for the job and lived there for a few years until I left to start my own company. I'm an only child, I like to roller skate, and I don't like tomatoes or carrots." She smiled sweetly. "Is that enough?

Dominic chuckled. "It's a start." He'd noticed a slight bitterness that crept into her voice when she mentioned leaving the defense company to start her own business, but decided to ask her about that later.

"What about you? I know a lot about your professional life; tell me something about yourself that I can't Google, something more personal."

"Well," Dominic fortified himself with a sip of bourbon, "As you have probably heard from Sheridan, I am the youngest of six kids. Well, technically, the next youngest; I have a twin sister, Nicollette, and I am older than her by four minutes. But we are the youngest. My family is from New Orleans, but we moved to Shreveport when I was three, so that's where I and Nicollette grew up. My parents moved back to New Orleans after my grandfather died ten years ago, and my father took over his surgical practice."

"Before or after Katrina?"

"Before, unfortunately." Dominic sighed heavily at the memory. "They lost the house where the rest of my siblings grew up in the hurricane. It was the same house that they'd bought when they got married, so my parents were devastated. Still, they, my brother Grant, and his wife Diana--who was still alive then--made it to Atlanta during the evacuation. My parents went on to stay with Camille in Baltimore, and Grant and Diana left Atlanta to stay with some of her relatives in Houston. Nicollette and I were still doing our residencies at the time."

"Did Grant's wife die?"

"Yeah. A car accident, over six years ago. He never remarried. No children."

"I'm sorry to hear that."

"Yeah. Diana was great. Grant loved her a lot; sometimes I wonder if he'll ever get married again."

Taryn tried to break the somber silence that had descended upon the table. "You have five surgeons in one family. How, or why, did you all choose that path? Sheridan never talks about it much, though she seems to speak highly of your late grandfather."

Dominic snorted in derision. "She'd be the only one." Dominic swirled his bourbon around in his glass. "Medicine, or more specifically, surgery, is the Bastille family business. My grandfather was one of the first surgeons of color back in New Orleans, and created a way of suturing called the Bastille Technique. It's still used around New Orleans today, mainly among the old-school surgeons. He drilled medicine and excellence into my father and his brothers; all of them became physicians, but only my father became a surgeon. My aunt, my father's sister, was a nurse. My mother was also a nurse; that's how she and my dad met. They worked in different departments at the same hospital. She retired after Nicollette and I were born."

"Your family gatherings must be interesting. Do you all swap copies of medical journals around the dinner table?"

"Ha ha." Dominic grinned as the server brought their appetizers. "It can get a bit intense when we all get together, but mostly we try not to let medicine dominate our adult private lives as it did our childhood. It's easier among the siblings than when we're with our parents."

"Do you see your family often?"

Dominic shook his head as he bit into a crab-stuffed mushroom. "As you may imagine, it's hard for us all to get together given our respective schedules and geographic locations. Medicine doesn't stop for holidays, and we tend to get busier during Thanksgiving, Christmas, New Year's, and the Fourth of July. Still, we make it a point to try and get home for our parents' anniversary, even if it's just for twenty-four hours. And we almost always make it home for Mardi Gras; well, except Nicollette. The siblings, though, we video chat with each other as a group, once a month, and on holidays. Technology is a true blessing for our family."

The rest of the dinner was filled with laughter, especially when Dominic and Taryn exchanged career stories. There was also a growing aura of physical attraction, which was not lost on either. The spell was briefly broken when the server came by with the dessert menu.

"I'm not sure I can eat another bite," Taryn complained as she browsed the menu.

"You should try. The crème brulée here is insane, as is the white chocolate cheesecake and the chocolate fudge cake."

Taryn gave him a scrutinizing look. "You must

come here often, if you've sampled most of the dessert menu."

"Not that often, but enough to know what's good," Dominic admitted with a sheepish grin. While the restaurant was out of the way, he liked going there because he could eat his meal in peace, with just a book for company. He decided to omit that he'd taken Nell here before, when they dated.

"Can you cook?" Taryn asked after the server took their dessert orders.

"I make a mean grilled cheese sandwich." At Taryn's skeptical look he said, "Seriously, that's pretty much all I know how to make, besides spaghetti. I lived on both of them during my senior year of college, when I moved off campus into my own apartment. It was a 15-minute walk from campus, and over twenty minutes to the cafeteria. When the wind chill was in the negative numbers or it was snowing, I was not trying to go out in that kind of weather just to eat."

Dessert arrived and Taryn wasted no time tucking into her crème brulée. "Oh my God, this is so good," she moaned.

Her moans put all sorts of pleasurable images in Dominic's head. He tamped them down by focusing on his own dessert. "I told you it was good."

"I almost always get the crème brulée every time I come here, but it's always on point. "She smiled at Dominic as she cracked the caramelized sugar crust and scooped up a partial spoonful of the sugared brownness. "Still, an excellent suggestion."

Dominic couldn't help but stare as Taryn licked the spoon clean, her eyes half shut with pleasure. His groin tightened and he was glad he was sitting down, and that the tablecloth extended halfway to the floor. "Uh, did you want to try some of my cheesecake?"

"Sure. Cheesecake is on my list of favorites."

Dominic cut off a piece of cheesecake with his fork and held it in front of Taryn's mouth. She looked at him curiously before parting her full lips and allowing Dominic to slide the fork in. Taryn savored the rich, creamy texture of the dessert, never breaking eye contact with Dominic.

"Good?" Dominic asked in a quiet tone.

"Good," Taryn confirmed.

They finished their desserts in a haze of sexual tension. Dominic paid the check and they left the restaurant. "I'd love to take you to this little jazz bistro," Dominic said when they were in the car, "but unfortunately for me, it's a school night. Plus, the really good bands play on the weekends."

"You don't have to explain," Taryn reassured him as they sped back to her house. Once again, Dominic escorted her between the house and the car. He took Taryn's hand in his and held it until they were standing outside her door. Taryn held her palm up to the plate beside the door and leaned into the retinal scan. The locks snicked open.

"You have biometric locks on your house?" Dominic was amazed. "How?"

"I know people who did me a solid when I had the house built."

"But why?"

"I work from home almost as much as I work from the warehouse," Taryn explained. "I have projects that are worth hundreds of thousands, and maybe millions, of dollars. I don't trust an ordinary lock-and-key, or even numeric passcoded system. This is more secure." She grinned at Dominic's dazed expression. "I had a really good time tonight, Dominic. Thank you."

"The pleasure was definitely mine," Dominic replied. "Maybe we can do it again. I could take you to that jazz bistro."

"I'd like that."

Taryn pushed open her door; Dominic followed but stayed in the foyer. They stood in silence for a few seconds, his hazel eyes boring into her brown ones. "Well, good night."

"Good night, Dominic."

They watched each other for a few seconds more. "I'm going to kiss you now," Dominic finally said.

"Okay."

Taryn had been kissed before; some men knew what they were doing, while others made her want to suggest remedial lessons. Dominic, she had to admit, was a professional. The moment his lips touched hers, Taryn felt the sensation down to her toes. And when he parted her lips and slipped his tongue inside, she wanted to whimper with pleasure, but it came out as a moan.

Dominic had kissed many women during the course of his lifetime, but none of them had affected him like this. It was as if he needed to breathe and Taryn's full, sensual lips were the pathway to oxygen. He cradled her face in his hands and deepened the kiss, wanting to get as close to her as possible.

Taryn instinctively pressed herself against Dominic and wrapped her hands around his waist. She could only react, as her brain had short-circuited from desire minutes ago. *If he kisses like this, I could just imagine what he'd be like in bed.*

Dominic's hand crept over Taryn's hip to mold

around her generously rounded bottom. He pressed her closer and figured she could feel his hardness against her soft belly, but he was too lost in her kiss to apologize or even care. She was a grown woman and should understand that these things happen.

They continued to kiss until the sound of a throat clearing penetrated their sensual haze. They broke apart to notice a man shooting a disapproving glance as he walked his dog past the house. Neither Taryn nor Dominic had shut the wooden front door behind them, and their liplock was clearly visible through her glass screen door . Taryn and Dominic exchanged a grin.

Dominic traced a thumb across Taryn's swollen lips. "I'd better go."

Taryn noticed the question in his eyes and knew that he'd stay if she asked, but one-night stands weren't her thing. And she wasn't trying to add herself to the list of Dominic's conquests. "Yeah, I think that's best."

If this were anyone else, Dominic would have been ready to charm his way into a few carnal hours, but something inside him wanted more than a quick roll in the hay with Taryn. He dipped his head for one last kiss, savoring the taste of Taryn before backing away. "Bye." He fumbled with the screen door and was glad to take in a lungful of the cooling nighttime air. He needed to get his mind right before he attempted to navigate I-85 at night. As it was, Taryn would be on his mind during the drive back to Atlanta, and long after he'd gotten home.

"Bye." Taryn watched until he got in his car and drove away, then closed and locked the door. She leaned against it to catch her breath, a grin plastered across her face. She walked upstairs entered her room on shaky knees and pooled heat between her thighs. Dominic Bastille was a piece of work.

## 6.

Three days later, Taryn and Dominic were on a video conference. "Good to see you again, Taryn," he greeted with a grin. "I was beginning to think that you were avoiding me."

Dominic had called and texted Taryn every day since their dinner and subsequent kiss. Taryn wasn't sure where she wanted all this to go, so she buried herself in her work and let his calls go to voicemail, and his texts unanswered. However, she'd reached a point in the mock sim where she needed more technical information, and for that she had to go to the source.

Taryn ignored his question. "I need some more technical information about transplantation, the actual ex-vivo technique, stuff like that, so I can finish this mockup." Since he was only visible from the chest up, Taryn could see that today's outfit included a cream-colored V-neck sweater over a yellow dress shirt and a brown-patterned bow tie.

Dominic leaned back in his chair. "You know, I can always drive up there and give you the information you need."

Taryn raised an eyebrow. "I'm sure you have other things you should be doing."

"Part of the perks of being the boss is deciding my own priorities." He gave Taryn a hopeful grin.

"Not today." She bit back a grin at his brazenness.

"Can't blame a brother for trying. Alright, lay 'em on me. What are your questions?"

For the next hour, Dominic took Taryn through the basic techniques of an organ transplant, and outlined the specifics for kidney and liver. He even described the ex-vivo technique and how his research tweaked it for organs other than livers.

He was telling her of a strange case on which he'd consulted when there was a brief knock on his door. Before he could say "Come in," Cecily breezed in. "Knock knock..." her voice trailed off as she saw Dominic's glare. "Oh. I'm sorry. Am I interrupting?"

"Yes." Dominic's glower spoke volumes.

"I have all of the information I need, I think." Taryn heard Cecily's voice, and did not like the look on Dominic's face due to Cecily's appearance. She was not trying to get caught up in whatever power struggle these two had going on, which seemed steeped in their history with each other. "Dr. Bastille, thank you for taking the time to help me with my research. I'll be in touch once I've finished the mockup."

"Anytime. You know how to reach me if you need anything else."

Cecily's eyes had narrowed at the back of Dominic's computer when she heard Taryn's voice. She stared at Dominic, trying to determine if he gave a double entendre or not in his parting sentence to Taryn.

As soon as the video chat ended, Dominic exploded.

"What the fuck is your problem, Cecily? How many times do I have to tell you that you do not barge into my office whenever you feel like it? I was on a business videoconference! My door was closed for a reason. I could have also been in a meeting with another doctor, or someone else."

Cecily was unnerved in the face of Dominic's ire. "But you weren't," she blurted.

"And how the hell would you know?" Dominic's face was a mask of anger. "You are supposed to have access to my calendar for business purposes only."

"I am here on business!" She looked down and smoothed the front of her orange silk wrap dress, to gather her thoughts.

"Really? What kind of business?"

"I...." Cecily thought fast for a good excuse. "I came to tell you that Baxter Pharmaceuticals is interested in funding some of your research."

"They already fund some of my research."

"Well, they want to fund more of it."

"Now that's interesting, considering that when I spoke with my Baxter liaison earlier this morning, he didn't mention anything about additional funding." Dominic folded his arms across his chest and waited for Cecily to tell her next lie.

"Well, they will, after they read about your new project in *Healthwatch Today*." She peeked up at Dominic's face to see if he bought her fib.

"Uh huh." Dominic's tone dripped disbelief.

"What is this really about, Cecily?"

Cecily played with the large costume citrine ring on her right hand. "What is going on with you and that Taryn woman?"

Dominic couldn't believe his ears. "I beg your pardon?"

"What's going on between you two?" Cecily put her hands on her hips. "There's something between you two, and it's not just business. I can feel it."

"I can't believe this shit," he mumbled under his breath. Aloud, he said, "I'm not doing this with you, Cecily." He turned to go back behind his desk.

"*You owe me, Dominic.*"

Dominic turned back incredulous. "I what?"

It was Cecily's turn to glare. "You owe me."

"How you figure? I paid what was owed on the cancellation fees for the wedding and reception. You kept the ring. You went on our honeymoon trip to Fiji alone. And I let everyone believe that you dumped me, instead of the other way around. So how, exactly, do I owe you?"

Hurt tears gathered in Cecily's eyes. "You son of a bitch." She turned on a brown snakeskin high heel and wrenched the door open. She almost bowled Lori over as she stormed out of the office.

Lori looked at her rapidly departing figure, then entered Dominic's office with a nonplussed expression. "What happened, Dr. Bastille? How did she get in here?"

Dominic just shook his head. He was still trying to figure out what Cecily meant by he owed her. He pushed it aside and concentrated on Lori's presence. "What's up?"

"Your three o'clock consultation is here."

Dominic nodded and rose to slip on the lab coat that hung on the back of his chair. He'd figure out Cecily's drama later, and try not to think about how his day had started out so well and had gone sour so quickly.

## 7.

Later that evening, Dominic was on the phone with his brother Ted. He recounted a tale of a fundraiser dinner he'd been suckered into attending, and how a local politician tried to get the Atlanta Transplant Consortium to endorse his run for mayor of Atlanta--and for each of the executive team members to give a hefty donation.

Ted chuckled as he shook his head. "That's why I leave all that gripping and grinning to you physician types. It couldn't have been me."

"Yes, it could have been you," Dominic reminded him. "You had the highest MCAT scores out of all of us. Medical schools were throwing offers at you like confetti at Mardi Gras."

Ted snorted. "And end up in Grandfather's crosshairs? No, thank you. One of the smartest things I ever did was to tell him and his obsession with 'legacy' to kick rocks. And the look on his face when I told him I was switching my major to nursing in college." Ted's smile could best be described as vengeful. "It was a great moment in history."

They both remembered that Sunday dinner during Ted's sophomore year in college, which was also Dominic and Nicollette's senior year in high school. Dominic thought that Grandfather had been about to stroke out at Ted's news.

"Yeah, it was. But you know, for all his rage and disappointment, I think Grandfather respected you for standing up to him. None of us were ever able to do it."

"None of you ever tried," Ted corrected. "He had all of us quaking in our boots. I just got tired of it." He changed the subject to something more pleasant. "So what's up with your love life these days? Hotlanta is crawling with good-looking, educated, professional women. I know you have sampled the wares down there."

"I have, and it's been interesting. But between women trying to lock me down with an MRS degree, and Cecily trying to block, it's been a bit of a challenge."

"Cecily who?"

"Cecily Porter. My ex-fiancée."

Ted's light brown eyebrows raised in surprise on the other end. "Stop. Wait. Reverse the tape. How did Cecily end up down there? I thought she was still back home?"

Dominic explained how shortly after he arrived in Atlanta--and, of course, after he'd already signed his contract and received his signing bonus--Vincent, the CEO of the ATC, announced that their new Director of Public Relations, Cecily Porter, would be joining them at the beginning of the following week due to her relocation from New Orleans.

"You knew Vincent from medical school, right?" Ted asked.

"Yeah. But he was never about actually practicing medicine. He's always been about that executive life. I think he went to medical school because his dad paid for it, even though his dad was head of a health insurance company."

"Do you think he knew about you and Cecily before he hired her?"

"I don't know. I find it hard to believe that he couldn't find a qualified public relations director here in Atlanta, where there are so many major corporate brands, universities, and professional sports teams. I can't figure out why he'd import Cecily from out of state, and have to pay her relocation fees on top of what I am sure is probably a nice, six-figure salary."

"She may have had Dr. Porter to pull some strings,"

Ted pointed out.

"That crossed my mind too, not that Cecily doesn't have talent. But doing a solid for the head of the Porter Foundation would be just the foot in the door that Vincent would break his neck to get." Dominic rubbed the back of his neck in frustration. "I can see moving here because that was truly the best move, professionally, but she could have gotten better, more prestigious offers in places like Washington, DC, New York, even San Francisco or Miami."

"Stop ignoring the obvious, Nick; that girl moved to the A for you."

"But why? It's been over three years since we called off the wedding. I thought she'd moved on."

"I'm surprised that you're surprised that Cecily is still in love with you."

"You may be onto something, there. Earlier today, she interrupted a video conference I was on with...with someone who's working on my research, and when I went off on her, she threw a fit and told me that I owed her."

"Was this someone female?"

"Yeah. Why?"

"Well, there you go. Cecily was jealous and trying to block." Ted paused. "Was there something that needed blocking?"

"Maybe." Dominic exhaled deeply. "Okay, I'm not really surprised. I just hoped that if I ignored Cecily, she'd go away."

"Didn't I teach you anything? When you cut things off, cut them off firmly and clearly. Less drama that way." Ted paused, then asked, "Why did you break off the engagement, anyway?"

"I didn't break it off; Cecily did."

"Sell crazy somewhere else. The only way Cecily would have broken off your engagement was if she'd met an untimely death." When Dominic didn't answer, Ted continued. "Well, you'll talk about it one day, I guess. But for you to break things off, there must have been a damn good reason. I mean, you had the sweet setup: nice-looking wife, well-connected father-in-law, your pick of hospitals, maybe even eventual Chair of the Porter Foundation. To walk away from that, things must have gotten pretty bad. And since you're still suffering in silence over the issue, let's change the subject. Do you know how many women have asked me to set you up with them?" Ted shook his head in amazement. "You'll need a catcher's mitt for all the new booty coming your way."

"I hope you turned them down."

"I did, because word on the curb is that you've been otherwise occupied."

Dominic frowned. "Who told you that?"

"The grapevine is small, little brother. Word back home is that Miss Cecily Porter is none too pleased with the attention you've been paying to the woman who's doing some work for your research project. I assume she was the 'someone' on the video conference?"

"Touché," Dominic admitted.

"It has also been said that you took this woman to the Porter Foundation gala. And, Sheridan let it slip that y'all went out on a date."

"Sheridan needs to mind her own business."

"I see. This woman cute?"

"Does it matter?"

"Yeah, she's cute. Cecily wouldn't be tripping if the girl was ugly. So what happened?"

"What do you mean?"

"She's cute, you're single, I assume she's single, which means you tried to take this beyond the professional."

"Touché. I took her out to dinner. And I had to kind of finagle that, under the guise of a working dinner, since she didn't want to mix business with pleasure."

"And?"

"And what?"

"Did she give you dessert?"

"The cheesecake at the restaurant was quite good."

"Oh, so you're playing dumb, now. Must be something special about this one."

"Whatever."

Ted raised an eyebrow. There was something special about this one, even if his brother didn't want to admit it. He decided to play a hunch. "When did Cecily throw her fit, again?"

"Earlier, in my office."

"And you were on a videoconference with this woman, correct?"

"Yeah. Taryn needed a step-by-step of the transplantation and ex-vivo processes, so she could finish the mockup sim for my project. So?"

"Taryn? That's her name?"

"Yep. Taryn McIntyre."

"Hold up. You're kicking it with T-Mac?

"We're not kicking it," Dominic said in exasperation. "I figured Sheridan would have given you all the pertinent details."

"Sheridan can be very close-mouthed when she wants to be." Ted chuckled. "I gotta hand it to you, you could do worse than Taryn."

"You know Taryn?"

"Yeah, I know Taryn; we met a few times whenever I visited Sheridan in college, and they swung up to UVA once to roll with me and the bruhs. She's good people, easy on the eyes and smart as hell. I didn't make the connection because you never told me her last name, and last I knew of Taryn, she was working in California."

"Well, she's in the Atlanta area now, working on my project."

"And you really don't see the connection between Cecily's recent behavior and Taryn? Come on, Nick. We men tend to be oblivious, but not that oblivious."

Dominic finished his beer and placed the empty bottle on his coffee table. "You're right," he sighed. "I didn't want to see it, because that meant I'd have to deal with Cecily and her ever-hurt feelings."

"About time you caught up."

"Incredible," Dominic muttered under his breath.

"So what are you going to do about Taryn?"

"Do?"

"Yeah. Are you going to go for that, or what?"

"I don't think she'd go for it. She was very clear about not wanting to mix business with pleasure." However, Dominic was not so sure that Taryn meant to stick to her guns on that, after the kiss they'd shared.

"I'm telling you, little brother," Ted advised, "you have to use the tools of the trade to get the girl."

"What am I supposed to do, ask her if she needs a kidney?" Dominic snapped.

Ted sighed. "You're being too literal. Look, she needs research for your project simulations, right?"

"Yeah. But she's already done a lot on her own, and I've given her a lot of information as well."

"You have to do more," Ted urged. "So take her around, show her a day in the life, take her to your lab. Laboratories are aphrodisiacs; ask Camille."

Dominic chuckled at the reference to their eldest sister Camille's inadvertent slip about having sex in her laboratory with her now-husband Andrew, while they were dating. "I'm not trying to sex her in my lab."

"Why not?"

Dominic shook his head. His elder brother had always been somewhat of a hound, and the years had not mellowed him out any. "Anyway, since you're giving all this advice, what's up with your love life?"

"It's good."

"I take it you haven't settled down yet?"

"Let's just say I'm celebrating diversity. But this isn't about me, it's about you. What are you going to do?"

"I don't know. But that day-in-the-life thing has

some merit."

"I know it does. And you can parlay that into dinner to discuss the day's events then, if you play your cards right, you can show her your bedside manner up close and personal."

"Taryn's not like that."

"And how would you know?"

"She's just not."

Ted was glad that Dominic couldn't see his grin. It had been a long time since his brother had been protective of a woman in a positive way, which meant that Cecily Porter was finally out of his system. He was so pleased at the thought, Ted contemplated attending Mass on his next day off to give thanks to the Almighty. "Well, play it as it lays, then. But you have to get Taryn on the hook so that you can reel her in."

"Yeah, yeah."

The impatience in Dominic's voice told Ted that he'd grown tired of this conversation, so Ted decided to switch the subject to more neutral territory. "Let me know how it goes. So what do you think of the Saints' options in the upcoming NFL draft?"

## 8.

Taryn looked around with interest as the camera crew scuttled to and fro in preparation for the upcoming taping. Dominic was doing a one-hour video segment about his ex vivo technique for a cable medical show, and he'd invited Taryn to watch as part of her research for the simulations. She stood to the side so she wouldn't be in anyone's way and had to admit to herself that the experience was kind of cool. She looked over to one corner of the room, where an actual makeup artist was dabbing at Dominic's face with foundation to make him show up better on camera. She waited for a break in the human traffic and dashed over to where Dominic sat with a pained expression on his made-up face.

"Well, don't you look pretty," Taryn teased.

"Don't start," Dominic warned. Had he known that the video segment would include wearing foundation, he would have opted out.

"Look up toward the ceiling," the makeup artist instructed as she wielded a dark-tipped pencil.

Dominic eyed the pencil with suspicion. "What's that?"

"Eyeliner."

"Jesus," Dominic mumbled as he cast his eyes toward the speckled ceiling. The makeup artist deftly darkened the rims of his eyes, then stepped back and studied her handiwork. "Looks good, Dr. Bastille," she said with a self-satisfied nod. "You're ready for the camera."

Dominic examined his face in the mirror and shook his head. He hadn't signed on for all this. What self-respecting surgeon went into the operating suite in full face? Granted, some of his female colleagues wore makeup on surgery days, but only one came fully made up to work every day, surgery or not.

Cecily came over, picking her way through the snaked cables across the floor. Vincent Behane, the ATC's CEO, was right behind her. "All set, Dominic?" she chirped.

"This is going to be great for ATC," Vincent gushed. "You'll be glad you did this, Dominic. This is part of the growth I promised you when you came on board."

"We'll see, Vince," Dominic replied. Vincent had always been somewhat of an attention whore, even in medical school. In fact, he'd thought that Vincent would make a good match for Cecily, if she'd let it happen.

Cecily's cheeriness dimmed when she saw Taryn.

"Oh. Hello, Taryn. I didn't know you'd be here." She shot a questioning glance at Dominic.

"I invited Taryn so that she could get a better idea of what I do and how I do it, for the sims."

"I'm glad you could come down," Vincent said as he shook Taryn's hand with a grin. "I've heard about what you've done with the mock simulations; Dominic can't stop raving about them. I can't wait to see the finished product." His brown eyes gleamed with excitement and greed. "ATC is going to really give Emory a run for its money!"

Cecily's pursed coral lips demonstrated her displeasure at Taryn's praise, even as her grey-blue eyes took in Taryn's khaki cargo pants, solid-colored red Keds sneakers, and long-sleeved red T-shirt. She dismissed Taryn and turned her attention back to Dominic. "They're almost ready to start shooting." She reached out to smooth down an errant strand of hair and managed to keep her smile pasted on her face when Dominic jerked his head backward and glared at her.

Dominic was all too glad when the video director called for everyone to take their places. When Cecily had told him of the offer to do a video segment about the ex vivo technique for a new medical show on cable television he saw not just a professional opportunity, but also one where he could implement Ted's suggestion to use the tricks of the trade to get Taryn interested in him in a non-professional way. The first kiss they'd shared after their lone dinner was shaping up to be their last if he didn't do anything about it; Taryn was sticking to her "no business mixed with pleasure" mantra. She was as stubborn as he was, which added an extra thrill to the chase. Of course, Cecily wouldn't be Cecily if she didn't try to block. If Cecily would just stay in her lane as the PR Director, things would be fine, but Dominic had no hopes of that. He was not in the mood for her shenanigans, not when so much was at stake.

"Places!" the director called out. He adjusted the headset that rested atop his faded green baseball cap and squinted into the monitor of a camera. He waited until Dominic joined the group of residents that had agreed to be part of the documentary. "Quiet on the set! And...action!"

Dominic tried not to squint from the camera lights. He turned to his group of residents, all of whom were dressed in scrubs, as he was. The show's narrator, Brittany Schroeder, was similarly attired and part of the group. "Today, we're going to perform the ex-vivo repair of a kidney that is slated for transplant. The kidney was found to have slight damage due to the donor being hypertensive, but the overall kidney function has not been compromised. We are going to remove the kidney, repair the damage with ex vivo, then transplant it to the recipient, who will be prepped and waiting in another operating suite." He surveyed his residents. "Now, who can tell me what ex vivo means?"

"Ex vivo simply means 'outside of the body," one of the residents answered, her bespectacled eyes darting nervous looks at the camera. "It's when an organ is repaired outside of the body, instead of inside it as usual."

Dominic nodded. "Correct. For many transplants, especially lung transplants, a damaged organ cannot be used and is thrown away. Using the ex vivo technique and a synthesized tissue patch I grow in my laboratory, I can remove the damaged organs from the organ donor, repair them, and transplant them to a recipient. The tissue patch is twice as durable as the organ tissue, yet because it is organically grown from living tissue, the chance of the recipient's body rejecting the repaired organ is drastically reduced."

"Dr. Bastille," Brittany asked, "do you have a patent on this technique?"

"Yes, there is a patent pending."

"This must be thrilling, following in your

grandfather's footsteps," Brittany continued. "After all, Dr. Lucien Bastille was the creator of the Bastille Technique of organ suturing."

Dominic managed to keep a frown off his face. He hated being compared to his grandfather, or any reference to the Bastille Technique; he wanted to be known for his own works, not trading off his grandfather's name. "I was fortunate to have such an exemplar growing up."

Taryn noticed the tic in Dominic's jaw when she mentioned his grandfather. She remembered Dominic's snarky comments about his late grandfather and hoped that the narrator would move on from Lucien Bastille, if she wanted this video to progress smoothly.

Brittany caught the chill in Dominic's voice at the mention of his grandfather and quickly switched the interview to more neutral ground. "How do you teach this to your residents? Do they get to work with you in the lab as well in the operating room?"

"I select a second- or third-year resident every year to assist me in my research. While the Atlanta Transplant Consortium is not a hospital in the traditional sense, we do open our doors to teaching, and we have an arrangement with local medical schools. Medical students are allowed to observe surgeries in our gallery, and residents are allowed to participate if they have proven themselves." He looked at Brittany, then at his residents. "Let's move on. We have a lot to do today."

The camera crew, along with Taryn, Cecily, and Vincent, followed Dominic as he lectured a group of residents who were training for a subspecialty in organ transplantation, then shot Dominic in the surgical suite as he actually repaired a damaged organ with the ex vivo technique. Brittany got to interview the resident working in Dominic's lab, who explained how the patch tissue was grown. Dominic was also filmed interacting with nurses and other doctors. They were allowed to film from the observation gallery as Dominic actually transplanted the repaired kidney into a 23-year old man in end-stage renal disease, who would have probably died waiting for an undamaged one. Finally, Brittany was allowed to interview the family of the transplant patient and Dominic's post-surgical discussion with them. The filing ended with a shot of Dominic at his desk in his office, reviewing a chart as he was surrounded by files and papers.

"And...cut!" the director yelled. "That's a wrap, people. Dr. Bastille, thank you so much for allowing us to glimpse your groundbreaking medical techniques." He grinned and nodded at the cameraman. "We got some good stuff."

"When will the segment be aired?" Cecily asked.

"We still have to edit, then get it to the network, so about six weeks or so. You can call the station in a couple of weeks to get a more definitive date and time."

Cecily nodded as she and Vincent exchanged pleased looks. Dominic walked over to where they stood. "So, what did you think?"

"I think it was awesome!" Vincent's smile was wide enough to show the silver molar near the back of his mouth. "This is going to really help propel ATC into the stratosphere. Well done, Dominic."

"It went really well," Cecily concurred. "You're going to need another executive assistant to field off all the offers that are going to be coming your way. Teaching opportunities, speaking engagements, staff positions at other institutions..."

"Dominic doesn't need to worry about positions anywhere else," Vincent jumped in with a nervous grin. "Dominic, make sure you tell them that we've got you locked up for the next five years. With stock options!"

Dominic merely smiled. During his contract negotiations, he made Vincent include a one-year early opt-out clause for the next five years, although if he opted out after three years, he forfeited any type of severance or stock options. With Dominic's salary, though, the loss of such wouldn't hurt him. Vincent had good reason to be nervous; there was nothing from stopping Dominic from leaving ATC if a better opportunity came along.

Taryn watched the back and forth with amusement. The video segment had gone much better than she had expected, even with Cecily and the CEO of the ATC hovering in the background. She'd taken a lot of notes on her smartphone, and already her mind was buzzing with ways she could tweak the sims to really make them sizzle. She was itching to get back to her computers and start programming, but she didn't want to be rude.

Dominic must have read her mind. "Taryn, could you wait up a bit, please? I want to speak with you about something."

"Sure."

He walked over to the makeup chair, where the artist quickly removed his makeup. Dominic rose from the chair in relief and left the room.

Taryn watched as the last of the cameras were packed and the crew left, and gathered her own things. Vincent left after a quick word with Dominic but Cecily hung around, obviously waiting for him as well. When Dominic returned from changing back into his office attire, she walked up to him, hips swaying, and linked her arm in his. "Hey, why don't we go celebrate the taping? There's this new bistro that people are raving about, and..."

"I already have plans tonight, Cecily."

Cecily paused, an embarrassed flush creeping up her cheeks. She shot a look at Taryn, then back at Dominic. "Oh. Of course. Well, if you don't need anything else, I'll be heading home. Give me a call later."

"I'll see you tomorrow at work."

Cecily looked as if she'd sucked a lemon. "I see. Well, see you tomorrow." She stomped out of the room as fast as her tight suit skirt and four-inch heels would allow.

Dominic turned to Taryn. "Ready?"

"For what?"

"For dinner. I'm starved."

"All that filmmaking worked up an appetite?"

"Something like that. But I also overslept this morning, so I only had time to grab a banana and a cup of coffee."

"I thought you had plans?"

"I do: with you. Unless you have other plans?"

Taryn blushed at Dominic's boldness and thought of what she had on tap for the evening: more coding on a new video game she was developing, as well as mapping out the changes she wanted to make to Dominic's sims. "Nothing I can't put on hold for the evening."

"Cool." Dominic led Taryn out of the room and to the parking lot.

Taryn's Tesla was parked two rows down from Dominic's Audi A6. "You want me to follow you?"

"Hmm. How about we drive back to my condo, so that you can park your car in the garage of my building? It'll be safer there. Then we'll leave from there to get some grub."

They did just that, and Taryn alighted her car in the underground garage and walked over to where Dominic's car was now parked. "I thought we were going to dinner?"

"We are, but I want to change into something more comfortable. Do you mind?"

"No, that's fine." Taryn had to admit that she was a bit curious to see how Dominic lived.

They took the elevator up to his level, and walked down the hall to his unit. Taryn noticed that there were only four doors on the floor. When Dominic unlocked his door, Taryn shook her head and smiled.

"What's so funny?" Dominic asked as he pushed open the door and ushered Taryn in. His security alarm beeped a warning.

"I haven't used a metal key to open or lock anything in a long time."

"Oh?" Dominic finished punching in the alarm code and the beeping stopped. "How does that work?" He gestured for Taryn to have a seat in the living room.

"You saw my work setup, and my house is a smart house. And my car, of course. My life runs on computers." Taryn sank down onto the caramel leather sofa, over which was thrown a black and gold crocheted throw.

"So you're basically screwed if the power goes out."

"Pretty much," Taryn agreed in a cheerful tone.

"I'll be right back. You want anything to drink before we go?"

"Nope, I'm good." Taryn watched Dominic retreat into a doorway down the hall, then let her eyes roam around the room. It was tastefully decorated with caramel leather furniture in the living room over a beige, red, and blue patterned rug. The fireplace looked functional and had logs arranged for the next time he decided to light a fire. The hardwood floors were a honey color and were covered with other, large carpets that matched the one in the living room. The kitchen had gray granite-topped counters and an island; bar stools were pulled up to the outer counter, which could serve as an extra eating space. The dining area boasted a rectangular walnut table that shone beneath the low-key hanging fixture and was accented by six high-backed upholstered chairs with red and blue-patterned slipcovers. A woman had definitely had a hand in decorating this house; maybe this was all Cecily's work.

Dominic returned wearing relaxed straight-legged jeans, loafers, and an untucked gold shirt with small black symbols patterned across it. He finished buttoning the wrist of his left sleeve. "I'm all set. You ready?"

"Yep. You have a lovely home."

"Thank you. Or rather, thank my twin sister Nicollette; she was kind enough to fly out from San Diego to decorate the place for me after I closed on it. I'm not good at stuff like that. If it was up to me, I'd be sleeping on a memory foam mattress in front of a huge flatscreen plasma TV that was hooked up to my PS4."

They took the elevator back downstairs to the garage and got in the car. "So, where are we going?" she asked as Dominic pulled out of the garage.

He turned down a street packed with stores and restaurants. "What are you in the mood for?"

"Surprise me."

They ended up at a small restaurant that was known for its seafood. After an excellent dinner, they left the restaurant and Taryn turned in the direction of where he'd parked the car. Dominic snaked an arm around her waist and guided her in the opposite direction. "Where are we going? The car's that way," Taryn asked in surprise.

"The day's not over," Dominic replied. "In fact, we still have," he paused to check his watch, "four hours and thirty-eight minutes until it is officially tomorrow. Consider this further continuation of a day in the life of Dr. Dominic Bastille."

"The video segment has been over."

"It can't hurt to have more research, right?"

Taryn raised her eyebrows. "You're mighty bold, Dr. Bastille."

"My mama told me that a closed mouth don't get fed. "

Taryn looked up into his mischief-filled eyes. "Alright, then."

"Good, because I'd hate for you reschedule whatever you had going on. I would have written you a doctor's note, though."

Taryn tried hard not to burst out laughing. "That's good to know."

"I aim to please." He led her into a video arcade, where they were immediately assaulted by bloops, bleeps, whirs, and the sounds of laser shots. Dominic looked like a kid in a candy store as he scanned the machines that ringed the room. "Hey, there's a pinball machine open."

They spent the next hour playing pinball, where Taryn lost most of her games. She had a tendency to move her entire body when she played, rocking the machine in the process and sending the pinballs other than where she wanted them to go. At one point, Dominic stood close behind her and placed his hands over hers. "You're fighting the machine," he spoke in
a low voice in her ear. "Just relax and let the balls come to you."

Taryn's pulse sped up at the sound of Dominic's voice in her ear, and the thought of his balls coming to her in a more intimate way. He was dangerously close to her erogenous spot, behind her earlobe, and her panties were already wet enough. She shifted her head slightly and tried not to think of how well his body meshed with hers. His hands moved hers over the pinball flippers with a dexterity that belied their appearance, and the effect was even more arousing. She wasn't the only one to feel it, judging from the slight hardness in her lower back.

The ringing of the machine's alarm and the flashing red light indicated that she'd won the game and three more pinballs, but she was ready for the game to be over so she wouldn't throw Dominic atop the machine.

Dominic felt Taryn's heart rate increase when he spoke into her ear. He was tempted to nibble her earlobe but didn't want to move too fast. It was hard for him to concentrate on the pinball game, as Taryn had a habit of grinding her firm, rounded rear into his pelvis each time she tried to hit the ball with the flipper. He thought about an upcoming budget meeting to relieve the hardness in his pants. When the game ended, he was relieved that he'd averted disaster, though he had a feeling that Taryn would be the equivalent of a category 5 hurricane in his life, if he wasn't careful.

He stepped away from Taryn and stuffed his hands in his pockets to hide any traces of his erection, grateful that he wore his shirt untucked. "Did you want to play something else?"

Taryn looked around the room for a safer game to play, one that wouldn't lead to increased physical contact. She spotted the pool tables in the back of the room. "Do you play pool?"

"Do I play pool? I'm the best in three parishes, *cher.*"

Taryn snorted. "We'll see. And we're not in Louisiana. Rack 'em up."

Taryn waited while Dominic racked up the balls in the center of the pool table and chose her pool stick. Dominic leaned on his own stick, watching Taryn in a way that made her feel like she was the last chicken wing on the plate and he hadn't eaten in a week. She quickly turned her attention back to the pool table to hide her lustful thoughts.

Dominic couldn't help but admire Taryn's rear as she bent over to take shots. He also couldn't help but notice the way she arched her lower back when she was about to hit the ball. The movement fired his imagination: Taryn on all fours, arching to receive him as he entered her from behind, grabbing her shapely hips as he slid in and out...

"Six in the side pocket."

Dominic snapped back to the present as Taryn called her next shot. He shifted and held the thin pool stick in front of him, leaning on it and praying that his shirt covered his painful erection.

Two games later, they were tied with a win apiece. Dominic checked his watch; he knew he should be headed to bed, but he didn't want to be in his bed tonight without Taryn in it too. He looked at Taryn with a devilish grin. "Let's up the stakes for the tie breaker, shall we?"

Taryn frowned in suspicion. She did not like that glint in Dominic's eye. "What kind of stakes?"

Dominic's grin widened. It could even be described as wolfish. "We play for kisses."

"What?"

Dominic laughed out loud at the look of pure shock on Taryn's face. You'd think he asked her to strip naked and dance on the pool table. Which was a nice thought, but one step at a time. "Every time you miss a shot, I get a kiss. Every time I miss a shot, you get a kiss."

*Oh my God.* Taryn was not ready for this. Pool was supposed to be a hormonally safe game for her. But Dominic was determined to write a check she was a bit nervous about him cashing.

Dominic waited for Taryn to respond. He knew she was hesitant, but he had to apply a full-court press. He thought he'd missed his chance when Taryn avoided him after their kiss over a week ago. Now that he had a second chance to be with her, he was going to milk it for all it was worth. He just had to get Taryn on board. He decided to appeal to her competitive nature. "Unless you're scared?"

"I am not scared!" Indignation drove away any fear. She hadn't backed down from a challenge since she was four years old, and you didn't make it far in her field unless you had some killer instincts--especially if you were female. Taryn's nostrils flared as she placed a hand on a hip. "Let's do this."

Dominic racked the balls, Taryn broke first and a striped ball dropped in a corner pocket. "Stripes," she announced and proceeded to make her next three shots. Her fourth shot bounced off the side and went wide of a pocket. Taryn straightened, took a deep breath, and turned to face Dominic.

Dominic walked around to her side of the table. He could see that Taryn was nervous but determined to hold up her end of the bargain. He could also see by her parted lips that she
wanted to kiss him as much as he wanted to kiss her. Dominic stepped close and decided at the last minute to kiss her on the forehead, so as not to overwhelm her. Taryn, however, had other plans.

Taryn lifted her head and rose up on her toes to meet Dominic's lips. They were as soft as she remembered them to be. Heat pooled between her thighs as Dominic's tongue dueled with hers.

Dominic had been all set to take things slower but

Taryn must have read his true heart. The moment her lips touched his, he needed more. He deepened the kiss, feeling oddly like he'd come home. He moved his hands over her hips and drew her closer.

Taryn felt Dominic's hardness against her belly and pressed closer to him. She locked her fingers behind his neck, straining to get closer. She needed to be closer...

Wolf whistles snapped Taryn out of her lustful haze. She pulled away from Dominic, her face flushed and her lips swollen. Dominic wiped his mouth with a sheepish grin as another patron shouted, "Get a room!" Laughter erupted at the comment.

Dominic shot Taryn an inquisitive look. "Do you want to finish playing?"

Propriety dictated that Taryn insist upon them finishing their pool game. The heated throb between her thighs dictated something else. She took a deep breath and said, "No. We can leave."

Dominic searched Taryn's face. He studied the pouty lips he'd feasted on mere seconds ago, then looked into her big brown eyes. He saw the desire underneath the apprehension,
and nodded. "Let's go."

The drive back to his condo was quiet. Once inside the foyer, Dominic kissed Taryn with a renewed ardor. Taryn dropped her purse and wrapped her hands around Dominic's back, trailing her hands up and down his spine. Their tongues dueled and it was a battle that Taryn was glad to concede.

Dominic trailed hot kisses down the side of her neck as he fisted his hands in her locs. Taryn threw her neck back in pleasurable abandon as Dominic moved lower to fasten upon an erect nipple. He suckled her through the fabric of her long-sleeved T-shirt before he needed more. He slipped his hands underneath her shirt and broke the kiss long enough pull it over her head. Her jeans followed. Dominic feasted on Taryn's heaving breasts that strained to burst from her purple lace bra, and shapely hips barely covered in matching boy shorts. His erection pressed tightly against his zipper as Taryn looked him in the eye, unclasped her bra and shimmied the straps off her shoulders before letting it fall to the floor. Taryn's breasts stood proudly upon their release, almost begging Dominic to continue his ministrations. He recaptured Taryn's nipple and was rewarded with a throaty groan.

Groaning was all that Taryn could do as she became lost in the magic of Dominic's tongue. Her hands pulled Dominic's shirt up of their own volition; she needed to feel Dominic's skin next to hers. Dominic's shirt joined her clothing on the floor and she ran her fingers through the thick hairs on his chest. She placed a trail of kisses down his chest until she reached the hardness behind his zipper. Taryn unbuttoned his jeans and used her teeth to pull down the zipper. Dominic's breath caught as Taryn stroked him before pushing his jeans and boxer briefs down. Dominic quickly stepped out of his clothing and stood in all his naked glory. Taryn's eyes roamed across his athletic build with visible pleasure.

The corner of Dominic's mouth ticked up in a smile at the examination. "You like?"

"Oh yes." Taryn reached for him. "Let me show you how much."

They came together in another heated kiss. Dominic backed Taryn into the caramel leather sofa and eased her down upon it. He kissed down to her tropical warmth and tasted her wetness. Taryn's back arched in a rush of intense sensation as Dominic feasted upon her. She flung one leg over the back of the couch to give him better access and moved her hips restlessly. Dominic sucked and licked as the spicy pressure in Taryn's womanhood built, then peaked. She came with a shudder and a scream as her body was awash in waves of pleasure.

Dominic winced slightly at Taryn's tightened grip on his hair, but the pain was a small price to pay for Taryn's responsiveness. He rolled off the couch and retrieved a condom from an enameled box on the coffee table, donned it quickly, and slid into Taryn while she was still in the throes of her aftershocks. Taryn gasped aloud at Dominic's swift entry and wrapped her legs around his back. She raised her hips in rhythm to Dominic's thrusts, quickly coming to a second, much stronger orgasm. Dominic's completion arrived with a growl a short time later. They lay glued together in sweaty, sticky satisfaction as their heart rates slowed.

Dominic retrieved the black and gold throw from one end of the sofa and spread it over them. He shifted so that Taryn nestled comfortably against him and they lay in companionable silence. Taryn traced a finger through the swirls of black hair on Dominic's chest, coming to terms with what just happened. She didn't regret sex with Dominic at all--she hadn't had her back cracked quite like that in a long while--but she did think about possible repercussions with her job. She'd narrowly dodged a bullet with Michael five years ago; if this got out, she could easily be kicked off the project.

Dominic felt the tension ease into Taryn's body. He kissed her on her forehead, tasting the light mist of salt on her skin. "What are you thinking about?"

Taryn hesitated, then answered, "I was thinking about my job. I could land in a lot of hot water if this ever got out."

Dominic raised an eyebrow. "How would this get out, unless either of us says something? I don't know about you, but I don't kiss and tell."

Taryn chuckled and raised her head to plant a kiss on Dominic's lips. "I don't kiss and tell, either. And while I can't really be fired unless you do it--since you're the one bankrolling my work on your project--it just looks bad. It looks unprofessional."

"How is that anyone's business, as long as it's consensual?"

"That's easy for you to say, because you're a man. You can sleep with whomever you want with few, if any, repercussions; people will still see you as a brilliant surgeon and medical researcher. But as a woman, my professionalism and expertise will immediately be called into question, and it could affect my getting any future projects."

"I disagree, but whatever." Dominic shook his head and held her tighter. "Well, you won't have to worry about that happening." He gave her a long, searing kiss. "How about we compromise your professionalism a little more?"

Taryn's laughs turned to purrs as Dominic captured her attention for the next hour.

Much later, they were snuggled in Dominic's king-sized bed. Dominic twirled one of her now-damp locs around his finger. His mind drifted, and a thought came to mind. "You're 36 and no kids?"

Taryn raised an eyebrow at the abrupt and out-of-the-blue question. "Nope. No dependents."

"Is this by choice?"

"Yep. I assume I can have children because there have never been any fertility issues on either side of my family but since I've never been pregnant to my knowledge, I can only guess. Although there are quite a few only children among my cousins; but that was by choice."

Dominic mulled over that for a minute. "Did you ever want children?"

Taryn shook her head. "I thought I did, when I was younger. But that was because of how I was raised; it was automatically assumed that I would grow up, go to college, get a good job, get married, have children. It's what was done among my family and peers."

"You ever think you'll regret not having them?"

"No. I like my life, Dominic. I like being able to

pick up and go whenever and wherever I please, without having to hustle for a babysitter, or a family-friendly locale. I like sleeping late and staying up later. I like having the disposable income to do whatever I want. Plus, me being childless is good for the environment," she joked. "My carbon footprint is drastically reduced." She tilted her head up to look at Dominic. "What about you? Aren't you at the stage in your life where you should have the requisite 2.5 kids and a house with a white picket fence?"

"Not me. I'll leave all that to Camille; she likes traditional stuff like that." He shifted his shoulder to better accommodate Taryn's head. "I opted out of the reproductive market a few years ago, after my engagement was over."

"You had a vasectomy?"

Dominic chuckled at the surprise in Taryn's voice. "Is that so strange?"

"Well, yeah. Most men rely on women to handle birth control issues, so as to keep their masculinity intact."

"Oh, so you're doubting my masculinity now?"

It was Taryn's turn to chuckle as she slipped a languid hand beneath the covers. "Not at all," she drawled, cupping him in her hand.

Dominic grinned and guided her hand back up to his chest. "Girl, I'm tired. You wore me out."

Taryn gave a bark of laughter. "Yeah, right."

"Seriously. I'm not as young as I used to be."

"Whatever, Grandpa."

"Anyway, back to what you were saying. I have a niece or nephew on the way, so I can get vicarious parenthood that way. And, as a bonus, I can give him or her back when I'm done spoiling them and feeding them a lot of sugar. It's a win-win."

"But you never wanted kids?" Taryn propped herself up on one elbow and looked down at Dominic.

"Nope. I have five brothers and sisters and even though Grant and Camille were gone for most of my and Nicolette's childhood, I remember how it was a bit of a struggle for my mom and dad. They never seemed to relax much; Dad was always working and though Mom retired when Nicki and I were born, we were a handful." He paused, lost in memory. "People think that because my dad was a doctor, that we were rolling in it. Yes, we were afforded some privileges that others may not have had on a daily basis, but it wasn't all roses. We had to work part-time jobs if we wanted pocket money, and we had each chores to do. Then there was med school, and seeing how the students with families had to do this constant juggling act between home and school. It was harder on the women than the men, and especially the single parents. But they all struggled." He shook off the memories. "Anyway, I pretty much figured out that parenthood wasn't for me., but I didn't decide to actually do something about it until years after that revelation."

"So you got snipped after your engagement ended?"

"Yeah. I wasn't ready to be a dad, and I hadn't figured on going back down the marriage road again, so why not?"

Taryn privately wondered if Cecily had been on board with his no-baby plan, but decided not to ask. "I feel you on not being ready to be a parent. It takes a level of sacrifice that I don't know if I have in me."

"You sacrificed for your career," Dominic pointed out.

"That was different. That was on my terms and if I messed up, I had opportunities to self-correct on my own timetable. You don't get a do-over on a child's life. I don't want that responsibility."

"You ever think you'll change your mind?"

Taryn huffed in exasperation. "I am so tired of people asking me if I'll change my mind! 'You'll change your mind when you met the right man.' " Taryn's voice was mocking in its cruel mimicry. "Like I don't know my own mind, or what's best for me. If I haven't figured it out yet at the age of 36, then I'll never figure it out."

"Okay, okay! Truce." Dominic pulled Taryn closer and nuzzled her locs in an attempt to smooth her ruffled feathers, then rolled atop her. "I have obviously messed up, so I'm hoping for an opportunity to self-correct."

Taryn's response was delayed as his deft fingers parted her folds. "How were you planning to do that?" she breathed.

Dominic winked as he burrowed backwards beneath the covers. "I can show you better than I can tell you."

## 9.

Dominic sped up I-285 on his way to Taryn's office in Norcross. He had no idea what was going on, but the excited summons from Taryn made him think that she'd made serious progress on the simulations. From what he'd seen so far, his grant money was well spent. Taryn took his research in a direction even he hadn't anticipated. He kept an eye out for state troopers; he didn't want to be held up by a speeding ticket. He really wanted to see what Taryn had come up with this time. And, he was excited at seeing her again. They'd managed to get together a few more times over the past few weeks, and each time Dominic felt like a kid in a candy store. Something about Taryn had gotten under his skin, and he couldn't get enough. It wasn't just the sex; he'd been around enough to tell the difference between good sex and a good woman, and Taryn fit both criteria. He just enjoyed being with her, even if it was just sitting in the same room while she coded a program and he reviewed a medical journal. They had the kind of relationship where they didn't have to talk all the time; they just had a comfort level with each other that couldn't be forced. He'd never had it like that with Cecily, or any of the other women he'd dated over the years. And he liked it. A lot.

Taryn met him downstairs in the lobby of MacSim, as usual. The minute he was in the lobby, Dominic pulled her into his arms for a long, kiss. "Mmm, I needed that," he murmured after they finally broke for air. "I've missed you."

"You just saw me this morning," Taryn chuckled as she took him upstairs on the elevator.

"That was hours ago." Dominic managed to get in a good liplock before the elevators opened on the floor of the main offices. Taryn led him down the hall to the big door with the biometric lock that he'd seen on his first visit to the company, the one that was reserved for more sensitive projects and that they'd bypassed on his tour. Taryn put her palm on the plate near the door jamb and leaned forward for the retinal scan. Dominic was impressed at the security. "More biometric scans?"

Taryn nodded as the door swished open. "Only three people at this company, including myself, have access to this room, due to the sensitive nature of some projects."

"So if you show me the room, you'll have to kill me?" Dominic joked.

Taryn cast him a sidelong glance. "If need be."

The deadpan look on her face made Dominic wonder for a moment if she was indeed joking. Taryn was serious about her work, so there was a possibility that he could end up on the side of a milk carton if he mentioned anything he saw. Before he could change his mind, Taryn entered the room. Dominic hesitated, then followed.

Dominic looked around the room with curiosity. Everything was dark gray: walls, floor, ceiling, and looked to me made of something other than drywall. There was no furniture, not so much as a window. Nothing but blank gray walls. The room almost had the feel of an underground bunker, minus the foodstuffs and other items associated with long-term survival. Or the lead of a pencil. Upon closer inspection, Dominic noticed that everything had a slightly glossy sheen, and looked to be made of something other than the usual drywall. He walked over and touched the nearest wall; its slick surface was cool to the touch and didn't feel like a regular wall. "Is this a game room, or something?"

"Or something." Taryn went into an adjacent room and turned on the lights while booting up the computer console. Dominic peeked in the room; the console looked like it belonged in any of the *Star Wars* movies. "Go back into that room, Dominic."

Dominic complied and stood in the center of the room, feeling superfluous. "Is this the part where I get beamed up to the Starship *Enterprise*?"

"You got jokes today." Taryn must have switched on a microphone, because her voice echoed through the speakers set in the ceiling. She was busy at the console. Dominic could see her body moving in concert with her hands through the large glass window that allowed her to look from the office into the room. "Dominic, I know that we're doing a standard simulation for your project, but I wanted to show you this." She finally sat down behind the console and took a deep breath. "Ready?"

"Lay it on me."

"Don't move."

Suddenly, Dominic stood in a surgical suite. His eyes widened at the masked and bonneted scrub nurses moving around trays of sterilized surgical instruments, the patient lying on the table draped in sterile surgical fabric and head covering, the heart monitor, anesthesia, and automatic IV machines beeping softly in rhythm to the colored lines and numbers on the monitors. Bright surgical lights shone down in selected spots. He looked down and saw that his hands were encased in sterile surgical gloves, and he wore a surgical gown over his scrubs. He felt the warmth of his breath against the scratchy surgical mask; a peek at his feet showed surgical booties over the sneakers he favored instead of clogs.

He took a step forward across the dark grey tiles of the surgical suite floor; this was surreal. A few seconds ago, he'd been standing in a blank, empty white room. What had Taryn done? He reached out a hand to touch the operating table; the coolness of the stainless steel permeated his glove. He moved his hand forward and touched the foot, then the arm and chest of the patient. They were solid and warm, and the patient's chest rose and fell softly in even, deep rhythms. He looked down at the open square area of skin on the patient's abdomen, framed in surgical sheets and painted brown with antibacterial solution. The patient was prepped for a kidney transplant.

Dominic reached over and picked up a scalpel, feeling its familiar weight in hand. Out of curiosity, he made a small incision into the skin of abdomen. Blood ran out and down the side, staining the surgical drapes. Dominic grabbed a square of gauze from the adjacent surgical tray and dabbed the wound. He held the stained material up in front of his eyes in disbelief, and touched a gloved fingertip to the stain. It smeared across the latex as he rubbed the finger against his thumb. The familiar, metallic smell of fresh blood hung in the air.` Dominic was stunned. This was as real as if he were actually standing in the OR of the Atlanta Transplant Consortium.

"Well, what do you think?"

Dominic's head snapped up at the sound of Taryn's voice. He looked around but couldn't see her among the masked figures. "What...what is this?"

"Holographic simulations. Just a little something I've been working on, as a private project."

"Are you serious?" But Dominic knew that she was, as serious as the holographic surgical suite in which he found himself.

"Yes. I haven't perfected it yet, which is why I'm not yet offering it to my clients. But I'm close. I wanted to try it on your sim because a surgical procedure would best fit with a holographic environment." Taryn peeked out the window at Dominic's stunned face and grinned. "So, what do you think?"

"This is hot!" Dominic's voice was filled with awe and admiration as he reached into the incision he'd made and felt skin and sinew separate at his probing finger. "Can you officially make this part of my project? Like an advanced course, or something?"

"Like I said, it's not perfect. Besides, it's expensive."

"I've got plenty of grant money left over. I want this."

Taryn chuckled. "We'll see." She touched a series

of buttons.

Dominic blinked rapidly as the surgical suite disappeared and he was once again in the empty gray room. He started at Taryn's re-entry into the room. "Taryn, you may have outdone yourself. For real. This," he swept his hand through the air, "this was freakin' amazing. The possibilities of teaching residents when there is limited OR time..." His voice trailed off as his imagination ran wild. "How much would it cost to build a room like this, and get the requisite computer equipment?"

"More than your grant budget," Taryn said as she shut down the room and prepared to leave. "I had friends help me build this from scratch, so I didn't pay as much. But a holographic room, plus equipment, will run you into the tens of millions. And, you'd need to hire someone to run it. That's a few hundred thousand more dollars." She led Dominic out of the room and firmly shut the door behind her. "It would be less expensive to get a bunch of holographic headsets."

"How much would that run me?"

"A few million, maybe ten, depending on how many headsets you want."

"Could you build them?"

Taryn shook her head as they went back to her

office. The arena of programmers was only a bit less frenetic than they'd been on Dominic's first visit there, but there was still a hum of activity. "I'm not that savvy. You should pitch your project to Microsoft; they've made a lot of inroads with their holographic headset. They might hook you up." She gathered her tote bag and shut down her computers.

"You done for the night?" Dominic was surprised. Taryn often worked until she ran out of steam, which tended to be in the wee hours of the morning.

"I could be. Unless you were heading back home?" She cocked her head to the side, a teasing smile on her lips.

Dominic snaked his arm around her waist. "I think I could find something to occupy my time on this end." They walked, arms around each other, until they left the building.

## 10.

"Guess what I got in the mail?" Taryn asked.

Taryn and Dominic were lounging in Taryn's double-sized chaise lounge in her living room. The Saturday weather was chilly and rainy, and they decided to just stay in. Dominic built a fire in the marble-mantled fireplace to ward off the chill. They'd just finished a game of the original *Empires of Kush* and were debating on whether to keep playing that game and going up the levels, or playing a few games of each installment. In the meantime, they were enjoying the soft heat of the fireplace.

"What?"

Taryn rose from beneath the red and white-patterned throw and retrieved an oversized envelope from the table in the foyer. She returned and held it out to Dominic. "An invitation to the annual Porter Foundation gala." She got back under the throw and snuggled closer to Dominic.

Dominic read the invitation; he had one just like it at home, though it was more of a formality in his case. "Interesting." Dominic handed the invitation back to her and wondered who put Taryn on the invite list; he doubted it was Cecily. "It's kind of a big deal at Atlanta Transplant Consortium, since Dr. Porter is a heavy donor. He even has a surgical suite named after him. So, are you going?"

"I guess." Taryn tapped the heavy, engraved, ecru invitation against her chin. "I'm not really one for galas and whatnot."

"Why not?"

"Because I hate dressing up, for one; and I hate all the butt-kissing, for two."

"It's not that bad. "Wait...yes, it is." Taryn laughed. "Seriously. I've attended for the past three years, and it's quite boring. Not that I would tell Dr. Porter that."

"Are you going?"

Dominic made a face. "I actually have to this year, since I'm now ATC brass."

"Aww, poor baby."

"Yeah. I've gone the past three years out of respect to Dr. Porter, and also because Cecily made sure I was there—on behalf of her father, of course."

"This Dr. Porter, head of the foundation, is Cecily's father?"

Dominic nodded. Taryn started to put two and two together. Dad was a major donor to the hospital, Dominic worked there, Cecily's torch for Dominic... "What's the deal with you and Cecily? It's obvious you two have some history." Taryn already knew the scoop from Sheridan, but wanted to hear what Dominic had to say about it.

Dominic sighed. "We were engaged once."

"Ah."

"You don't sound surprised. Let me guess: Sheridan opened her big mouth."

Taryn shrugged. "Cecily's behavior toward me had already let me know that something was up between you two, from the beginning. As for Sheridan opening her mouth, I didn't know it was a secret. I doubt she does, either."

"It's not, but..." Dominic shook his head in irritation. "I would have preferred you heard it from me. Anyway, we were engaged, and I broke off the engagement three years ago."

"What happened?"

It was Dominic's turn to shrug. "I didn't love her like I thought I did. Our families were acquainted with each other; her father did a surgical rotation under my grandfather, and Cecily was best friends with one of my cousins. We met, started dating, and I thought it was all good until I realized that Cecily was more in love with being Mrs. Dr. Dominic Bastille, than in love with me. And before my grandfather died, back when we were teenagers, he made it clear that Cecily Porter was a desirable mate for me. So I called it off about a month before the wedding."

"Your grandfather was matchmaking for you when you were still in high school?"

"Oh yeah." Dominic nodded.

"Wow. I'm sorry about that. Your broken

engagement, I mean."

"I'm not. I would have been miserable, and I can't live my life like that, like I was one of her purses or a collectible figurine: something to be admired on a shelf, a prized possession she could show off to her friends. Not that my grandfather would have minded. Excellence is expected of a Bastille." The last was delivered in a bitter tone.

Taryn's brown eyes were full of sympathy, and Dominic felt the need to explain further. "Don't get me wrong. I loved my grandfather, even though I didn't really like him, and medicine is a good fit for me. A good fit for most of my siblings, surprisingly. But Grandfather had very antiquated notions of propriety and family legacy. It was very important to him that my father and uncles follow him into medicine, and his grandchildren too. He wanted to build a Bastille medical dynasty in New Orleans and wasn't shy about it. He would always tell us that excellence was expected of a Bastille, so there were no excuses for bad grades or hanging out with anyone he deemed wasn't the right sort." Dominic tilted his head back to rest it on the back of the chaise, his eyes closed in memory.

"My siblings and I were encouraged by Grandfather to compete with each other; he tried to make us jump through hoops for his attention. Maybe that's why we're so close, because we stuck together against his misguided tyranny." Dominic reopened his eyes with a thoughtful look. "The funny thing is, my dad was glad to retire and let my brother Grant take over his practice. He tried to get out from under my grandfather's thumb by taking a surgical position at a hospital in Shreveport, but my grandfather's reach was long. He wanted his children around him and his fiefdom intact." He sighed deeply. "I don't think my dad ever really enjoyed surgery as much as my brothers and sisters and I do. He was good at it, and it kept a roof over our heads and food on the table, but he didn't enjoy it. He's much happier now, fishing every day on the bayou."

Taryn shifted so that she could look at Dominic. "How else has your grandfather's legacy affected you?"

"Well, I was determined to get out of Louisiana, for one. My grandfather attended Morehouse College for undergrad and Howard University for medical school. I went to Harvard for undergrad and Cornell for medical school. In fact, with the exception of Grant, all of us got the hell out of Louisiana as soon as possible, and as far as we were comfortable. Nicollette went to the most extremes: undergrad in San Francisco, medical school at Stanford, residency in Seattle, now living in San Diego.

She's totally West Coast."

"Don't forget your brother Ted, who's a nurse."

"Ted?" Dominic chuckled. "Yeah, he totally went off the reservation. I thought my grandfather was going to disown him. We tease him about being the black sheep, and the underachiever, but he may be the most fulfilled of all of us. He's happy being a nurse, and he's a damn good one. He runs a critical care unit in one of the best critical care hospitals in the country, and he's thinking about going the nurse practitioner route." Dominic sighed. "Being a Bastille ain't easy."

Taryn nodded in understanding, then switched the topic back to the original issues of the Porter Foundation gala and Cecily. "You do understand that she hasn't let you go, right? That Cecily still loves you?"

"I'm not completely dense, Taryn. I know that Cecily still has feelings for me, which is why I avoid her personally and as much as professionally possible. But Dr. Porter is friends with the CEO of the hospital, and has poured a nice chunk of change into ATC, so I have to tread lightly regarding my interactions with Cecily. And yes, it is not lost on me that Cecily uses that to her advantage." He winked. "They didn't name me Director of Transplantation because of my looks."

"Oh. hush."

Dominic loved watching Taryn smile. "So why don't we go together?"

"Huh?"

He laughed aloud at the shocked look on her face. "You're adorable when you're slow, Taryn. I said, why don't we attend the gala together? It's all your fault, anyway."

"What's my fault, and what does it have to do with the gala?"

"Weeellll..." Dominic drawled, "since you did such an excellent job on my sims so far--the progress of which has caught the ear of Dr. Porter since you gave Vincent and the rest of the Board a test run--I received a phone call from none other than Dr. Porter himself, making sure that I'd be in attendance. So you see, you owe me."

"I owe you?" Taryn shot him an incredulous look. "How you figure?"

"If you sucked at your job, I'd be able to fake the flu or something. Now, I have to sit and eat rubber chicken and rub elbows with surgeons *emeriti* who sit and talk about the glory days of medicine, back when dinosaurs roamed the earth and they whittled their own scalpels."

Taryn laughed. "Surely it's not that bad."

"Have you ever been in a room full of physicians?

It can get intense. One-upmanship is as much a part of the menu as the rubber chicken. Luckily, growing up in my family prepared me for all that nonsense."

Taryn was now used to the trace of bitterness in Dominic's voice when he talked about growing up in his family. He'd once shared with her that when Lucien Bastille died ten years ago, the funeral was a relief for him and his sisters and brothers. And his father, who had been in his grandfather's shadow all his life. "Well, I guess I'd better pay what I owe, then."

"I definitely plan to collect." Dominic shot her a lusty gaze.

Taryn returned it with an equally torrid one of her own. "I certainly hope so."

"How about a down payment?"

A corner of Taryn's mouth ticked up in a half-smile. "What did you have in mind?"

"A striptease would be nice."

"A striptease?"

"Yeah. Unless you want to give me a lap dance?" Dominic waggled his eyebrows up and down.

Taryn nodded, then got caught up in the spirit of the moment. She'd never done anything like this, but something about going outside her comfort zone was turning her on. She stood in front of the fireplace, the glow from the flames outlining her body. Taryn appreciated the heat at her back as she grabbed the hem of her sweatshirt and slowly raised it, keeping her eyes steady on Dominic's. Dominic was treated to the unveiling of her smooth abdomen, her "outie" belly button, the mole beneath her left breast. Taryn removed her top and tossed it aside to reveal a sheer pink-and-yellow bra. Her nipples stood at attention through the thin fabric.

Taryn ran a hand down her pushed-up cleavage and was rewarded with the lustful dilation of Dominic's pupils, rendering his eyes almost black. She pushed the straps off her shoulders one at a time, then moved her fingers to the front clasp. She undid the clasp and used the heels of her hands to push the bra cups aside while keeping her naked breasts covered. She paused. "Why am I the only one getting naked?"

Dominic grinned. "I asked you to strip for me, not the other way around."

"*Quid pro quo*, Dr. Bastille."

Dominic replied by ripping off his shirt before the words were completely out of Taryn's mouth. The monstrous hardness weighing between his thighs intensified as Taryn massaged her breasts before letting her hands fall away, giving him an unfettered view of her engorged nipples. "Is this what you want?"

"Oh yeah," Dominic replied in a strangled voice. "Keep going."

Taryn hooked her thumbs beneath the waistband of her gym shorts. Still maintaining eye contact with Dominic, she slowly shimmied the shorts down her thighs and stepped out of them. Her pink and orange, floral-patterned boy shorts hugged her ample hips.

"Take them off," Dominic ordered.

Taryn complied, revealing her full nakedness. She stood, hip-sprung, hand on one hip. "Your turn."

Dominic rose and removed his shorts and boxer briefs, revealing a huge erection.

"You got a license for that?" Taryn teased.

"It's what you do to me."

"Well, this is what you do to me." Taryn leaned back on the adjacent couch and spread her legs to reveal her wet womanhood. She trailed a finger down her abdomen to play with the bejeweled ring in her navel, then further to caress her wetness.

Dominic rose and placed his mouth at the entrance of her heated core, stroking himself as Taryn's back arched in pleasure. She grasped the sides of his head, urging him further into her depths. Right when she was at the brink, Dominic paused long enough to fish a condom out of the pocket of his sweatpants, don it swiftly, and enter Taryn with determination. The flames from the fireplace flickered across their entwined bodies, the rising and falling of their passion that was placed in bas relief by the heated light. The crackling of a piece of wood provided the soundtrack to Taryn and Dominic's moans, which crescendoed in time with the increased downpour outside.

Dominic and Taryn lay sated atop the sofa, letting the warmth of the fire dry their sweaty skin. Dominic reared up enough to push a few damp locs back from Taryn's face. He stared at her with a serious expression "What are we doing, Taryn?"

Taryn blinked, her eyes heavy with post-orgasmic sleepiness. "Huh?"

"What are we doing? Where is all this going?"

"Where is what going?"

"Us. I mean, we get together on weekends, but that's about it. I don't see you during the week unless it's about my project, and you're almost done with that. We talk, but not much since you're buried in your work. So what's up?"

"I have a business to run, Dominic. I can't just chase after you on a whim."

"I never said you had to chase after me. I'm happy

to stand still and let you catch me. But are you even in the hunt?"

Taryn frowned. "What's that supposed to mean?"

"It means that I don't have all of you. You're here with me for twenty-four, maybe thirty-six hours out of the week. We go out, come back home, have really good sex. And that's it. Not to mention, I'm usually here in Norcross; when was the last time you hung out with me in Atlanta? Or we took a trip somewhere for the weekend? And don't try to use your work as an excuse. There's something else going on."

"We've never gone on a trip for the weekend."

"Say the word, and we can. We can stay in the state, head down to Savannah or St. Simon's Island. We can hit New Orleans, you can meet my folks, if they're not traveling. Or we can go to Miami, New York, California, Toronto, Jamaica, Bahamas, Puerto Rico...let me know and I'll arrange it."

Wait...what? New Orleans? Parents? Taryn grabbed fistfuls of her locs in confusion. "Where is all this coming from, Dominic?"

"I don't know." Dominic sat up and stared into the fire, his face a reflection of the frustration that laced his voice. He'd never had this depth of feeling for any woman before--not even Cecily--and he didn't quite know what to do. Taryn wasn't making it easy for him, either; she could be hard to read and was rather independent. If he were honest with himself, Dominic had to admit that he wasn't used to women *not* falling at his feet, doing whatever he wanted them to do. He ran a hand across his damp hair. "I miss you, Taryn. I miss you when you're not around. It's not just the sex, although that's excellent." Dominic flashed a grin before his expression turned serious again. "I miss holding you. I miss your laugh, your smile. I don't know what's going on here, but I want to ride it till the wheels fall off. Feel me?"

"I..." Taryn wasn't sure. Things seem to be going a bit too fast all of a sudden. Then there were memories of what happened in California... She sat up and reached for her sweatshirt; this wasn't the type of conversation to have when naked.

Dominic saw the uncertainty on her face. "What? Look, if you don't feel the same way, then let me know. I'm a big boy; I'll live."

"It's not that. It's...I mean..." Taryn's hands gestured as she tried to find the right words.

Dominic had never seen Taryn so flustered. "What is it, Taryn? What can't you say?"

Taryn rubbed her hands across her face, trying to figure out where to begin. Because Dominic was correct:

she'd been holding back a large part of herself as a protective measure. She was surprised that he picked up on it, though she really shouldn't have been: Dominic had shown that he was remarkably sensitive to undercurrents and things left unsaid. If she weren't of a scientific bent, she'd say that he was borderline psychic.

"I feel you, just like I felt you a few minutes ago, Dr. Freaknasty." Her weak attempt at a joke fell flat and her grin faltered. "It's just that..." She exhaled sharply. "I was in a business relationship that turned personal, once. It didn't end well." She stopped short of saying that the relationship almost derailed her career, and it was through grit and luck--and a really good lawyer-- that she made it through to the other side.

"Okay," Dominic said slowly. He noticed the curt tone in the last sentence, and wondered what was behind it. "So you think that this," he gestured to himself and Taryn," is going to end the same way?"

"There are some similarities in the situations," she admitted. "So, yes."

"Well, what happened? In your other situation, as you put it?"

Taryn shook her head. "I don't want to get into that right now." She closed her eyes and tried to calm herself down; even after all this time, the thought of that dark time in her life agitated her. She softened her tone. "Maybe later on down the road, okay?"

Dominic saw, and felt, her agitation and wisely decided not to press the issue. "Fair enough. But I'll just state for the record: I'm not whoever he was. I'd appreciate it if you didn't paint me with the same brush."

Taryn inclined her head in acknowledgement of his statement. "Fair enough." Although she knew that time would tell if that were indeed true.

## 11.

Dominic entered the ballroom of the upscale hotel with Taryn on his arm. Taryn knew she looked good in the form-fitting deep gold silk gown with matching silk and chiffon stole, and Dominic was equally dapper in his tailored tuxedo with a black jacquard silk cummerbund and matching bow tie. She noticed the looks of appreciation, surprise, and envy from the other attendees, and knew that they made a striking couple. Dominic steered them toward a portly older gentleman with a tonsure of white hair that looked like spun cotton wool. Next to the man was a pissed Cecily, who was breathtaking in a black dress with jet and crystal beading that clung to a well-toned figure.

"Dominic!" the man cried as he pulled the younger man into a big hug.

"Dr. Porter," Dominic greeted. "Hello, Cecily."

"Dominic." She turned to her father. "Excuse me, Daddy. I have to check on the caterers." She left as fast as her four-inch, jet-beaded, strappy stilettos would allow, each step exposing a length of toned leg and thigh. Dominic knew why she was in a snit; she'd wrongly assumed that Dominic would accompany her to the gala and was very put out when Dominic told her he'd be taking Taryn.

Apology lived in Dr. Porter's watery grey-blue eyes. "I apologize for her behavior, Dominic. She is still..." he let the thought trail off as he focused on Taryn. "But that is irrelevant now. And who is this beautiful lady?" He took her left hand and kissed the back of it, not even blinking twice at the tattoos on display. Taryn smiled at the old-school gesture.

"Dr. Porter, this is Taryn McIntyre. Taryn, this is Dr. Alain Porter, founder and chairman *emeritus* of the Porter Foundation."

"Taryn McIntyre? Cecily's mentioned you, as has Vincent. You did Dominic's medical simulations?"

"I did," Taryn answered. Dr. Porter nodded.

"Wonderful work. Vincent can't stop singing your praises, and I had the privilege to see one of the simulations." At Dominic's raised eyebrows he admitted, "I shamelessly used my connection with Vincent to gain access to the mock-ups. I hope you'll forgive me, Dominic. I know how protective you are about your research, but I wanted to see what the hoopla was about."

"You could have just asked me, Dr. Porter. I would have taken you through a test run of the finished product."

"It's finished?" Dr. Porter looked at Taryn, who nodded, then back to Dominic. "Excellent!" He turned his attention back to Taryn. "You're going to make this young man very famous." He clapped Dominic on the shoulder with a grin. Dominic grimaced a bit; for a 67-year-old man, Dr. Porter still packed a wallop. "Maybe Dominic would then reconsider my offer."

"You don't give up, do you, Dr. Porter?" Dominic shook his head with a smile. "I'm happy where I am. Besides, I just got to ATC."

"Yes, yes, you're happy being a paper pusher, what with this promotion and all." Dr. Porter's tone was dismissive. "Granted, it's a nice feather in your professional cap, especially given your age. But I know you, Dominic. You miss the rush of cutting, of pure research. When you're ready to own up to that, call me. My offer still stands."

Cecily returned and linked her arm in her father's. "Daddy, Dr. Mofoyo of the Mayo Clinic wants a word."

"Alright, Pumpkin. Duty calls. Taryn, it was a pleasure meeting you and we must speak again. Dominic, I'll be awaiting your call." He let Cecily lead him through the well-dressed crowd. When they'd left, Taryn turned to Dominic.

"That was interesting," she commented. "He obviously thinks very highly of you, despite your broken engagement to his 'Pumpkin'. What's this offer he keeps dangling in your face?"

"He wants me to run the research arm of his foundation." Dominic placed his hand on Taryn's lower back and steered her toward the back of the room, where further conversation on the subject stopped as Dominic and Taryn paid their respects to Vincent and the other board members of the Atlanta Transplant Consortium. They circulated the room, with Taryn receiving kudos on her simulations and Dominic receiving praise for his performance as Director of Transplantation, as well as the strides he'd made in his research with the transplant sims.  Then it was time for dinner, and Dominic and Taryn were invited to sit at Dr. Porter's table with some medical luminaries and their spouses. Cecily shot daggers at Taryn throughout the meal, pausing only when she rose to introduce her father and the evening's speaker. Taryn was grateful that she didn't lose her appetite from all the negativity Cecily shot her way.

Once dessert had been cleared away, a five-piece band struck up a tune and couples took to the dance floor. Dominic rose and offered his hand to Taryn. "May I have this dance?" he quipped with a sparkle in his eye.

"You may." She took his hand and followed him onto the dance floor. Dominic wrapped his other arm around her waist and they moved about in an easy box step, nodding pleasantries at other physicians as they danced by. Taryn chuckled at the glances that trailed from her upswept locs, to the visible tats on her left arm, to her otherwise elegant attire. She, apparently, was a walking paradox to this crowd, and watching them try to figure her out gave Taryn even more amusement.

They left the dance floor after two more songs. Taryn fanned her face. "I'm going to freshen up. I'll be right back."

"I'll grab us some drinks. I'll meet you back at our table." Dominic gave her hand a quick squeeze before they parted ways. Taryn visited the ladies room, reapplied her lipstick, and felt refreshed enough to make it through the rest of the evening. Her mind was on an ice-cold glass of water when she bumped into a man right outside the hallway that led to the lavatories.

"I apologize..." Taryn's voice died as she recognized the man.

"Your apologies are never necessary with me, *querida*," Congressman Michael Tejada-Harris replied. His dark eyes drank in Taryn.

Taryn ignored the term of endearment. "You're a

long way from home, Michael."

"True, but I have some business interests here that may benefit my constituents back in California." He tucked an errant lock of hair behind Taryn's ear.

Taryn jerked her head away and glared at him. Michael chuckled, which further served to irritate Taryn. "I seem to be always overstepping my bounds with you, Taryn."

"Like you care."

"I care a great deal."

"Is cheating the new way to show you care these days? Someone needs to notify Hallmark, so they can make some greeting cards for the occasion."

Michael sighed and tucked his hands in his pockets. "I can say 'sorry' many times, because I was indeed sorry and pitiful. I would say it every minute for the rest of my life if I thought it would mean something." He looked at Taryn's expression of disbelief. "I made a big mistake, and I will regret it with my dying breath."

"You must not have regretted it too much. I hear you and Sylvia are engaged now."

Michael shrugged. "It is what it is."

Taryn raised an eyebrow. "Wow, that's a ringing endorsement of your fiancée."

"Everything is not as it seems, Taryn. But I see

that you are happy with your new man, the physician for whom you did the simulations." At Taryn's look of surprise he smiled. "Yes, I keep up with your career. Stellar work, as usual. I hear you've made quite an impression on the Atlanta medical community, and beyond. Your name is on the lips of many people here tonight." He gestured with his head toward the well-heeled crowd sitting at the round tables in the room. "Congratulations. This will be excellent for your career. I know you've worked hard for it, and suffered much."

Taryn nodded. "I have."

Michael hesitated, then said, "For the record, I would have protected you, if I could, back in California."

"No, you wouldn't have, Michael. It would have put your career in jeopardy, and you just couldn't have that."

"*Querida...*"

"Don't call me that! I'm not your *querida* anymore."

Michael nodded his head in acceptance. "*Oyamente.* Well, I won't keep you. I just wanted to say hello, and to congratulate you on your achievements."

"Thank you."

"Enjoy your evening." Michael bent down to kiss Taryn, but she braced his arms to keep him at length.

With amusement in his eyes, Michael changed the trajectory of his kiss to land on Taryn's cheek. She pushed past him and disappeared into the crowd. Michael's eyes followed her until he could no longer see her.

Dominic was finally walking back to the table with their drinks, after being stopped every few steps by well-wishers who had seen the video segment on TV, or had heard about his research. He saw gold shimmering out of the corner of his eye and knew it was Taryn. He turned to look at her, smiling, when he noticed her talking to a man near the restrooms. Dominic's smile faded when the man brushed a lock of hair off Taryn's cheek and behind her ear. It was a very intimate gesture, even though Taryn did not appear to be pleased by it. Still, she made no move to stop him, or the subsequent brief conversation, which disturbed Dominic. Who was that man and more importantly, who was he to Taryn?

~~~

Cecily swiveled her desk chair side to side as she tapped an ink pen in an irritated tattoo against her desk. She couldn't concentrate on anything; as usual, Dominic was foremost in her thoughts. Despite the end of their engagement over three years ago, Cecily had never stopped loving him. The fact that her father never blamed Dominic for it didn't help matters. Although if he knew what Cecily had gone through, he would have thrown a fit. A wave of sadness passed through Cecily and she sighed. Her baby--*their* baby--would have been three years old last week. She wasn't a fan of abortion-- she was raised a good Catholic--but there was no way that Cecily was going to be burdened with both the shame of a broken engagement and single parenthood. Not Alain Porter's daughter. She'd found out a few days before her final meeting with Dominic and was going to tell him, but he beat her to the punch and called off the wedding. Cecily refused to tell him and have him stay with her out of obligation. Besides, she'd always gotten the feeling that Dominic wasn't into starting a family, which was interesting given the large one from which he came.

While in Fiji on what should have been her and Dominic's honeymoon trip, she took a quick detour to Switzerland and had the procedure done with no complications and no fuss. The Swiss certainly knew how to keep their mouths shut, which Cecily appreciated. When she returned to the States and tried to pick up the pieces of her life back in New Orleans, she thought about telling Dominic, then decided against it. His fury would have known no bounds.

Cecily tossed down the pen and turned to look out her office window at the ATC parking lot. She was still fuming about the fundraising gala. How dare Dominic show up with that nobody to the fundraising gala for her father's foundation, when she--Cecily--was the one who put him on the map, publicity-wise. Not to mention, she still had plans to be Mrs. Dr. Dominic Bastille; getting Dominic on board was just taking longer than she'd planned. Though he'd broken off their engagement three years ago, she came to Atlanta in the hopes that he'd come to his senses by now. But this Taryn, this upstart, was trying to encroach upon Cecily's territory, and Cecily wasn't having it. Not when she'd spent the past year laying the groundwork to get Dominic back, which included getting her father to pull strings to get her the top PR job at ATC. Vincent was a medical school friend of Dominic's, and he'd always had a bit of a crush on Cecily, so she used that to her advantage when recommending that Dominic was the best choice to run the transplantation program at ATC. She did all this through her father, of course, so that it wouldn't come back on her. If Dominic had gotten the slightest whiff that she'd be working at ATC, he would have turned the job down and stayed in Newark.

Cecily tried to calm down by flipping through a

magazine. She paused at an article about Congressman Michael Tejada-Harris, the Democratic representative from San Jose,

California. He'd been at the gala, talking to Taryn and if Cecily's observation was correct, there was definitely some history there. She tapped a manicured finger against her Nars-painted lips, then picked up her office phone to make a call.

A few days later she found Dominic in the on-site cafeteria. He was dressed in scrubs, which meant he'd just gotten out of surgery, and was working on his lunch.. She sidled up to his table. "Dr. Bastille."

Dominic looked up when he heard his name. Wariness crept across his face when he saw it was Cecily. "Yes?"

"I'm still getting calls about your availability: interviews, medical consulting on talk shows like Dr. Oz," she said as she placed her tray on the table, across from him. "The video segment went over very well, and the network wants to talk about doing another. And, your mock simulations are getting a lot of buzz in hospitals."

Dominic went back to his meatball sub. "Tell them I'm busy," he said after swallowing.

"Now Dominic, you have to capitalize on your fifteen minutes of fame before they go away. Trust me, it'll happen sooner than you think." She nibbled on a slice of cucumber from her salad. "Taryn McIntyre is a master at it."

Dominic paused with his sandwich halfway to his mouth. "What are you talking about?"

"I'm talking about the lawsuit Taryn was involved in a few years ago; something about proprietary software. Makes me wonder if those simulation ideas are really hers. Honestly, if I had known, I would have persuaded Vincent to hire someone else."

"Vincent didn't hire her; I did. And everyone did their due diligence." Dominic shook his head and bit into his sandwich. "Jealousy is not a good look, Cecily. This is low, even for you."

"Despite what you may think of me, Dominic, I have always looked out for your best welfare."

"True, but that was because my best welfare was usually tied to yours."

Cecily was stung by Dominic's true words, which made her angry. "Really, Dominic? Then explain how Taryn dated Congressman Tejada-Harris for a year, which was coincidentally around the time he was introducing legislation that would have favored her heavily in her lawsuit. And how she got some really cushy projects on a freelance basis; projects for which, according to insiders, she shouldn't have even been considered. And then there was the matter of the lawsuit itself, which happened because she was dating a coworker; she claimed he stole her work for a project of his own, he alleged that she couldn't take no for an answer when they broke up. Strange, isn't it?"

Dominic eyed her over the rim of his soda cup. "You've certainly done a lot of digging to try and get something on Taryn. How far back did you go, again?"

Cecily frowned at his nonchalant tone. "You should be glad that I did, Dominic. If she created your simulations--your research simulations--on fraudulent technology, well...I don't have to tell you what could happen."

She watched Dominic's face and was pleased to see the doubt there. Dominic might not have cared about her feelings, but he cared a lot about his research and his professional reputation. If push came to shove and he had to choose between those and Taryn, Taryn would be out in the cold--which was right where Cecily wanted her.

The meatball sub sat like lead in Dominic's stomach as Cecily spoke. Taryn was a gifted developer and programmer, and her career success was due to that gift. But what if Cecily was right? Cecily, to her credit, was good at spotting these types of things; it took one to know one. And then there was Taryn's behavior with that congressman at the fundraiser a couple of weeks ago. What was that all about? Taryn wouldn't really discuss it when he'd asked her about it, only to say that he was someone she once knew. Then there was whatever happened in her past, with business--which she still wouldn't discuss. What was going on? And if it had a negative effect on his research...

Cecily speared a forkful of lettuce and went in for the kill. "I Googled Taryn's name myself, and saw some old news articles about the lawsuit. Unfortunately, the records are sealed and I got a sense that there was a nondisclosure agreement signed by all parties involved. Interesting that McIntyre Simulations was founded shortly after the lawsuit, which made me wonder if money changed hands. And a friend of a friend works for the congressman and confirmed his previous relationship with Taryn. Cecily swallowed her salad, checked her watch, and rose. "Gotta run. See you later." She waited until she'd left the cafeteria to let a victorious grin cross her face.

Dominic stared at the remnants of his sandwich,

deep in thought. He tossed the rest of his uneaten lunch in the garbage and forced thoughts of Taryn out of his head. He had a surgery that afternoon and he had to focus, even while his heart felt heavy.

~~~

The second video segment, which focused on Dominic's use of technology in his practice and his medical simulation project, officially aired during prime time on Tuesday evening, and by Wednesday morning Dominic's cell and office phones buzzed nonstop with congratulatory messages. His personal and work email inboxes were overflowing. Even Dr. Porter called to send his best wishes. Despite Dominic's broken engagement to Dr. Porter's baby girl, the old man respected Dominic's reasons for doing so and bore no hard feelings. He knew his daughter well.

Still, Dominic found it hard to feel elated. He glanced down at the folded page in the "Style" section of the local newspaper. Once again, jealousy rumbled in his gut as he looked at the picture of Taryn and Congressman Tejada-Harris. They looked quite cozy together and while it was probably a result of camera angles, the end result looked less than innocent. They even caught the congressman brushing back an errant lock of hair from Taryn's face and tucking it behind her ear, which Dominic saw happen with his own eyes. It was a very intimate gesture and that didn't still didn't sit well with Dominic at all.

Neither did a quick Google search on the congressman, which netted an article from seven years ago, when he was still up and coming. He'd worked for a Silicon Valley venture capital firm that had provided some financial backing for Taryn's first simulation project. There was mention in another article about their romantic relationship, and how it may have smoothed her way into some highly coveted tech projects, ones that may have been above her level of expertise and experience at the time. *Hmph! I thought she didn't mix business with pleasure so that her professionalism wouldn't be called into question.* He also looked up the articles about Taryn and the lawsuit, which was as Cecily had mentioned: alleged theft of proprietary information, Taryn portrayed as the vindictive ex-girlfriend, sealed records and a nondisclosure agreement by all. There was mention of a monetary judgment as well, but it was unclear who received it. Dominic stared at his computer screen, unsure of what to believe. Maybe Taryn was just as much of an opportunist as Cecily; the only difference was that Cecily never hid her true agenda. But surely Mark, at the very least, would have pulled Dominic's coat about it? He wasn't easy to fool and Vincent, for all his schmoozing, would have had Taryn checked out six ways from Sunday before bringing her on board.

He shook his head. Nothing made sense. He needed to talk to Taryn and hear it straight from the source.

A knock on his office door jolted Dominic from his negative train of thought. Lori escorted Taryn in and closed the door behind her. Taryn waltzed over and moved to plant a kiss on his lips. "It's official! Your virtual reality sims are ready to roll, and I emailed you the link so that you can go through them one last time before you take them public. Oh, and I talked to a friend of mine; he can help design holographic headsets for you at cost; that should keep you within your grant budget."

Dominic moved his head out of her target range. "Cool. Thanks."

Taryn raised an eyebrow at his lukewarm response, but said nothing. "I saw the second video segment last night. It was great! I knew it would be, since I was there when it went down and saw how you handled yourself and your residents."

"Yeah, it was pretty good."

"'Pretty good'? It was fantastic! You're totally blowing up, in a good way. And you deserve it."

"Thanks." Dominic turned his attention back to a stack of CVs.

Taryn was perplexed by Dominic's cool demeanor. "Are you alright?"

"Yeah. Why?"

"I don't know. You seem very standoffish all of a sudden."

Dominic shrugged. "Not really. I tend to distance myself from opportunists."

Taryn blinked in shock. "*Excuse* me? What's that supposed to mean?"

"I guess I was more helpful to your career than that Congressman, or that guy from your old job in California."

Taryn held up a hand to stop his hurtful words. "Hold up. Are you accusing me of sleeping my way to success? And of using them to get ahead?"

"Well, haven't you? You dated the congressman for a while, and that led to you getting some rather choice tech projects, which were rumored to be above your pay grade, at the very least. You dated that guy at your job, and maybe stole his ideas, but you got a nice settlement out of it, right? And you founded McIntyre Simulations shortly thereafter, so it all worked out well for you."

"Wow, you've been a busy bee, haven't you? Or

maybe Cecily was the one digging for dirt?" A twitch in Dominic's cheek told Taryn she'd hit the bull's-eye. "Yes, I dated Congressman Michael Tejada-Harris for a year. And yes, he introduced me to some people who could help further my career by dint of swinging some freelance projects my way. However, those assignments came because I'm damn good at my job, not because I slept my way to the top. I may have lacked practical experience, but I had talent and skills that trumped longevity, and my clients figured that out real quick. And in case you've forgotten, Atlanta Transplant Center called me before I even knew you were involved with the project--called me because of my formidable skills and vision, so I didn't need the Bastille name to open that particular door. And since you want to bring up the lawsuit, let's talk about that."

Dominic already felt bad for doubting Taryn, in light of her explanation. "Taryn, don't worry about it."

"No, you want to know so bad, so much that you're willing to listen to Cecily's poison, so you're going to hear about it." Taryn's hands were on her hips and her nostrils flared in anger. "I once worked for a military contractor. The military is doing things that are light years ahead of what is made known to the public. I got on with some really good projects, which helped develop my raw talent. Virtual reality and holograms aren't something just in science fiction movies; the government has been working on them for decades, and I was privileged to be there when it started gaining traction." She started to pace in front of Dominic's desk. "I worked long hours on the project with a guy named Cameron Mills. When you're the only people that you see on a regular basis, every day, well...things happen. Cam and I started dating on the low, and I thought it was going well. Until I discovered that he'd stolen some of my notes on a private project I'd been working on for my boss, who was different than his. He used that information as leverage into a more high-profile position on another project. Shortly after his promotion, he broke things off. When I put two and two together, I went to HR, and his boss, and my boss. There was a big stink and they tried to force me out of the company."

She closed her eyes and relived the humiliation and fear. "I knew I couldn't fight the company myself-- remember, they had lucrative government contracts and if this got out, those contracts would be jeopardized--so I asked Michael for help. He didn't want to get involved, as a lot of his campaign money came from veterans and other government contractors--but he secured a very good attorney for me, one that didn't have any direct ties to him, and paid for it. My attorney managed to prove my case, got me a nice financial settlement which helped launch MacSim, and got the records sealed so that it wouldn't come back to haunt me. And for the record, Michael and I broke up because he cheated on me with his campaign manager, to whom he is now engaged." She narrowed her eyes at Dominic. "Does that clarify matters for you?" She stopped, took a deep breath, and shook her head. "Where is all this coming from, Dominic? What's really wrong?"

"You once told me that you didn't mix business and pleasure, so that your professionalism wouldn't be questioned. Yet here we are; I mean, your simulations-- especially the holographic surgeries--would be a major feather in your cap if you pulled them off. You could write your own ticket anywhere, especially in the medical community.  Then, I find out that you also dated that congressman, who also helped boost your career. He wasn't shy about that getting out, since he was all over you at the fundraiser."

*"What?"*

Dominic ignored Taryn's shocked exclamation. "Look, if you're looking for someone with deep pockets, I'm not the one. I have enough women trying, women more skilled than you. So you can miss me with all that. I don't need the drama; I have enough going on in my life without having to watch my back in my personal life."

Taryn shook her head in confusion. "You're adding two plus two and getting twenty-two. You're way off base, Dominic. What's happened has nothing to do with our relationship."

Dominic snorted. He still hadn't looked at Taryn. "I doubt it. And for the record, we don't have a relationship. We had some good times in bed, but that's about it."

Taryn couldn't have been more hurt had he slapped her. She backed away from the desk and willed the tears in her eyes not to fall. "I don't know what your problem is, Dominic Bastille, but I'm not having it."

Dominic shrugged and tried to ignore the fury overlaid with hurt in her voice. "You don't have to."

Anger overtook the hurt. "Fine. Enjoy your new level of fame," Taryn spat. She spun on her heels and tore the door open, almost taking it off its hinges before she stormed out of the office.

Dominic rested his head in one hand. He thought that he'd feel better after exposing Taryn's deception, but he didn't. She sounded genuinely hurt and confused. What if she was telling the truth? No, Cecily knew better than to come to him without proof, and she'd sent him links to the stories. And, she'd spoken personally to the Congressman, who confirmed their previous relationship--hadn't she? Taryn hadn't broken any rules to be with Dominic; he was no one special to her. He was just another notch in her career belt. He was better rid of her. Then why did he feel so bad?

~~~

Dominic joined the prearranged video chat with his siblings.

"Well, look who the cat dragged in," Sheridan Bastille greeted. "Dr. Prime Time. Can I have your autograph?" She flashed a wicked grin as she opened a pint of ice cream. Her tablet was propped against the sugar bowl on her kitchen table.

"Shut up, Sheridan," he retorted as he reclined on his couch and leaned his tablet against his bent knees. "What's up Ted, Nicki, Grant?"

"Hey Twin," Nicollette Bastille answered with a grin. She propped her laptop against an oversized pillow and applied another coat of polish to her toenails.

"What's good, little bro?" Ted replied. He held his smartphone on his lap while he sipped a beer. "Did you follow my advice and seal the deal?"

"Seal the deal on whom?" Nicollette asked. "Is it the video game girl?"

"What video game girl?" Sheridan peered at the screen with concerned interest.

"You gave advice?" Grant shook his head in amusement. "The poor woman probably ran for the hills."

"What's wrong with my advice?" Ted asked in mock outrage.

"You have a tendency to get Cro-Magnon, Ted," Nicollette said with a chuckle.

Ted shrugged. "Some women like it. Anyway, so what's up with that, Nick?"

"Nothing. I've been real busy with work."

Ted raised an eyebrow. "Busy. With work."

Dominic ignored his rhetorical tone. "Yeah. And Nicki, the video game girl is the same one who did my sims."

"You played Taryn in video games? Ha!" Sheridan chortled with glee. "I know she whipped your butt."

Grant caught the shadow that passed across Dominic's face at the mention of this Taryn's name, as he participated in the video chat from the deck of his house overlooking Lake Pontchartrain. Though there was a ten-year age gap between them, he and Dominic had always been close. "You alright, Nick?"

"Just tired."

Nicollette looked at his face on her screen. In that

special way that twins share, she knew that it was more than work that was bothering Dominic, and it had something to do with this Taryn. Dominic had obviously had a falling out with her and needed to work it out himself, especially if he followed any advice given to him by Ted.

"Taryn got any friends around there?" Theodore pressed. "I'm overdue for a visit to the A."

"Why would Taryn subject any of her friends to you?" Nicollette asked.

"Because I'm an excellent catch, plus being the brother of the televised Bastille is giving me extra brownie points with the ladies."

Nicollette shook her head. "Just think of what you could accomplish if you used your powers for good."

"Bite me, Spawn. You got a man yet?"

Nicollette shot him her middle finger. Dominic turned the conversation back his way before Nicollette and Ted engaged in a shouting match. "Back to your question, Ted. Nothing's up. She finished the sims, and that was it."

That's it?" Sheridan's eyes narrowed. She hadn't spoken to Taryn in a few days but the last time she did, she'd indicated that things were going well with Dominic. Now, Dominic was acting like Taryn was someone he'd just met on the street. Something was up. "What did you do?"

"Nothing. Why? Did Taryn tell you that?"

"I haven't spoken to her lately and when we do speak, you're not the central topic of conversation. So again, what did you do?"

"Why do I have to be the one to have done something?"

"Because I know you." Sheridan fixed Dominic with a baleful stare.

"I didn't do anything!"

"You did! I can tell you're lying. It's okay to admit that you messed up, since I don't think actual grownup relationships are in your vocabulary. You wouldn't understand how they worked."

"I was engaged once, you know."

"And look how that turned out."

"Shut up, Sheridan," Dominic growled.

"Ooh, aren't we touchy?"

"You have to admit, you've been out there, Nick," Ted added. "Grown-up relationships really aren't your cup of Lipton."

"I think the term you're looking for is 'man whore', Ted," Sheridan added.

Dominic ignored Sheridan's baiting and

addressed Ted. "Spoken by the man who worked his way through a large grocery bag full of condoms during college."

Ted shrugged. "Safe sex is important. And you had your own bag when you went off to college."

"Only because you gave them to me."

"Alright, you three, settle down." Even though all of them were way past grown, Grant still had to flex his "eldest sibling" muscles once in a while to keep them in check. "As much as it pains me, Nick, I have to agree with Frick and Frack. Sounds like there's a little somethin' somethin' between you and this Taryn, beyond work."

"See?" Sheridan spoke again. "Even Grant noticed it, and he's not the most romantically inclined person in the world, especially since Diana died."

"Shut up, Sheridan," the others said in unison. Sheridan shrugged and went back to eating her ice cream.

Dominic clenched his jaw. "Well, I've been wrong before, so it doesn't matter."

Nicollette frowned. "Why doesn't it matter? What are you wrong about?"

Dominic shrugged. "She was just using me to help her career. That's all. And may have jeopardized mine in the process."

"What!" Ted exclaimed.

Dominic gave a quick recap of the information he'd found about Taryn's life in California.

"You're bent about that?" Sheridan scoffed.

" 'That' is no joke, Sheridan. If even a whiff of theft of proprietary information surrounds my research, I can kiss my grant money goodbye."

"And you think Taryn stole something?"

"Hold up, y'all," Grant admonished. "How do you know this, Nick?"

"I looked up the court case on the internet. There wasn't much, but all of the articles talked about the proprietary information, which was the crux of the trial. And," he sighed, "her congressman ex-boyfriend was at the Porter Foundation gala. Apparently, he swung some lucrative projects her way when she was starting out."

Sheridan raised her eyebrows in surprise. "Michael was there? Interesting."

Ted stroked his goatee thoughtfully. "You think she slept her way to projects?"

Dominic sighed and wiped a hand over his face. "I don't know. She says she didn't, but..."

Nicollette cut him off. "You actually confronted her about this?"

Sheridan shook her head. "How dense are you?"

"Wait a minute," Grant ordered. "Dominic, I hope you had concrete proof before you approached Taryn about this. You don't attack someone's career accomplishments without good reason."

Nicollette narrowed her hazel eyes, identical to Dominic's. Something didn't sound right about all this. "Nick, what gave you the impression that Taryn was using you to further her career?"

"Well, like I said, there were articles about her when I Googled..."

"No, Dominic. What made you decide to Google Taryn's past all of a sudden? This was never an issue before, and I'm sure that the board members of ATC did their due diligence on her professional background. And didn't you say that Mark endorsed her too?"

Dominic hesitated, then said, "Cecily spoke with someone who worked for..."

At the mention of Cecily's name, Dominic's siblings broke out in assorted groans and curses of disgust.

"Cecily's your source?" Grant frowned.

"You have got to be kidding me!" Ted swigged his beer to get the bad taste of Cecily Porter from his mouth. He'd always thought that Cecily just wanted to get her hooks into any Bastille, but Dominic happened to be the one available at the time, and the nearest in proximity. "Didn't we already have this conversation?"

"I'm surprised that you paid attention to anything she had to say." Sheridan replaced the lid on her ice cream with a decisive snap. "She likes to stir the pot."

"Takes one to know one," Nicollette teased. Sheridan flipped her the bird in return.

At that moment, Camille Bastille Paxson joined the video chat. Dark circles were heavy beneath her green eyes. A surgical mask dangled over the chest of her surgical scrub top. "Sorry I'm late. I got pulled into a surgery."

"What kind of surgery?" Nicollette asked.

"A window washer fell from three stories and broke his hip, leg, and arm in three places."

"Ooh, did they fix it with pins?" Sheridan asked, excited as she usually was when talking about broken bones. "I would have used..."

Camille cut her off. "I wasn't concerned with his bones, Sheridan. The break in his arm was impacting the radial nerve, so I had to go in and rectify that, and make sure he didn't have a brain bleed. So, what'd I miss?"

"Cecily is trying to start some mess between Dominic and Taryn, who is helping him on his research project, and who he is also dating ," Sheridan updated her elder sister.

Camille's light brown eyebrows raised in surprise. "You're dating Taryn McIntyre? And why would you listen to Cecily? She's still bitter that you broke up with her and thwarted her dream of marrying a Bastille."

It was Dominic's turn to be surprised. "You know Taryn too?"

"Well, she is my soror, Dominic; I met her when Mom and I went down to Spelman to see Sheridan cross. But she's made a name for herself here in the DMV." Camille used the local slang term for the Washington, DC/suburban Maryland/Northern Virginia metropolitan area. "We use some of her medical simulations here at Hopkins. She does good work."

Ted snorted. "You know Freak only rolls with state-of-the-art stuff so if she says Taryn has skills, she has skills."

"Some continuing education would do you some good, Ted," Camille snapped. It irked her when Ted called her "Freak", just because she'd succeeded very well academically, and at an early age.

"I happen to enjoy playing *Operation*," Ted quipped. "I still have my game from the second grade."

"The point is," Grant interjected to stave off yet another round of sibling sniping, "that you really need to take Cecily's information with a half grain of salt, Dominic. Google doesn't tell the whole story, and since when did you believe everything you read? Especially on the internet."

"And where were these articles published?" Ted added. "There's a big difference between
*The New York Times* and Gossip To Go.com."

"Did you even read the articles," Sheridan wondered aloud, "or did you just read the headlines and the little blurbs underneath them?"

"I want to know who Cecily talked to," Nicollette stated. "Unless she heard it straight from one of the people Taryn did projects for, or this congressman himself, I'd be a little suspect."

"I agree," Sheridan concurred. "As for the case information, how did you find that out? Those records are sealed; it was a closed trial, and everyone involved signed a nondisclosure agreement."

"Cecily is rather petty, " Grant chimed in. "She's like a little kid who breaks a toy so she won't have to share it: if she can't have it, then no one will have it."

"She's in PR, right?" Ted asked. "She spins stuff into another gravitational field for a living. It's as natural as breathing to her. Cecily probably couldn't state an undiluted fact if her life depended on it."

"That's probably how she got you to propose to her years ago," Sheridan co-signed, "'cause you certainly didn't love her."

Dominic started to tell Sheridan to shut up again, then closed his mouth; she had a very valid point. He had never really loved Cecily, not in the way a man should love the woman he was about to marry. He'd gone along with Cecily's "spin" on their relationship, hoping he'd become convinced it was true. He had a sinking feeling in the pit of his stomach as his siblings continued to take apart Cecily's "evidence". He thought back to Taryn's denial of his accusations and her own explanation, and felt even worse. Was Taryn really telling the truth? Did Cecily really bend the events so that he would end things with Taryn, knowing how he felt about gold diggers and social climbers? Did he make one of the biggest mistakes of his life?

"But Taryn looked kind of cozy with that congressman at the gala."

"They did?" Ted shook his head. "Damn."

"Did they both look cozy together, or was one more cozy than the other?" Sheridan asked.

"Huh?" Dominic scowled at her in confusion.

"Well, sometimes when I run into one of my exes, they make it a point to try and act all familiar because they realize that they'd made a mistake in breaking up with me. Their gestures are not welcome. And I know for a fact that Taryn left Michael, not the other way around."

Nicollette shot her elder sister an incredulous look. "Your ego is out of control, Sherry."

"Truth is truth. And define 'cozy': were they hugged up in a corner, or what?"

Dominic sighed. "They spoke briefly near the restrooms, where Taryn had gone. He
brushed some hair from her face."

"What did Taryn do?" Sheridan pressed. "Did she smile, giggle, touch him in return--what?"

"She kind of jerked back and gave him an ugly look," Dominic admitted. "But she didn't stop him, either."

"She probably didn't want to cause a scene over something so trivial," Camille said. "I've done that when I've ran into my exes in public. Like Sheridan, some of them get too familiar but it's not worth acting like I have no home training. It's usually best to cut things short and keep it moving." Nicollette and Sheridan nodded in agreement.

"You may have overreacted, Nick," Nicollette added. "Did you ask Taryn about him, or did you just up and accuse her without hard proof?"

The sheepish look on Dominic's face was not lost on his siblings, who collectively shook their heads at his error.

"Oh, Dominic," Camille sighed in disappointment.

"That was not the move, little brother," Ted added.

"You messed up, big time," Sheridan stated. Nicollette simply gave him a what-were-you-thinking look.

Ted continued to shake his head. "Jealousy is a helluva drug."

"I am not jealous," Dominic snapped.

"Yeah, you are." Ted shrugged. "Happens to the best of us."

Grant saw the despair on Dominic's face. "You know one of the good things about most people, especially those whom we love?" Because as sure as he knew his name, he knew that Dominic was in love with Taryn, even if Dominic didn't want to admit it.

"What?"

"We get a chance to rectify our mistakes, and ask forgiveness. And if we're lucky, we get to be forgiven."

## 12.

Dominic scrubbed out of the OR and was headed to the cafeteria for a long-overdue meal when a voice behind him called, "Dr. Bastille!"

Dominic turned around and saw Vincent leading a group of people. Among them was Congressman Michael Tejada-Harris.

"This is Dr. Dominic Bastille," Vincent introduced when the group caught up to Dominic and handshakes were exchanged. "He's Director of Transplantation Services here at ATC. Perhaps you saw his video segment last week on television?"

Some in the group nodded, including Michael. "It was quite an interesting interview." His voice was infused with hints of his mother's native Mexico. "Since I was in Atlanta on other business, I wanted to come and see things for myself. Perhaps some of your innovative transplant techniques with slightly damaged organs could be implemented in California."

"Congressman Tejada-Harris made a very generous donation to ATC via The Porter Foundation," Vincent added.

"Well, I'm still in clinical trials..." Dominic started but was cut off by Vincent.

"Speaking of clinical trials, perhaps the Congressman would like a tour of your lab?"

Dominic raised his eyebrows. "Now?"

Vincent ignored the incredulous tone in Dominic's voice and shot him a look that clearly said, *Do the tour. Now.*

Dominic wistfully thought about a sandwich as he pasted a smile on his face. "Of course. If you'll follow me?"

At the end the tour, the group chatted excitedly about what they'd seen in the lab and one woman, Michael's campaign manager Sylvia, strategized aloud as to how to use the basis of Dominic's research in streamlining organ donation rules. As the group carried the discussion onto an elevator, Michael stepped back and addressed Dominic. "I am having a get-together this evening for some people who are helping me here in Atlanta. I'd be honored if you came."

"Well, I'm not sure..." Dominic scrounged for an excuse for not attending; he really didn't want to be around one of Taryn's exes, and he had nothing in common with politicians.

Michael watched him, aware that Dominic was trying to beg off the invitation. "You won't have to stay long. There is a matter that I wish to discuss with you privately. After that, you are free to leave or stay, as you prefer."

Now Dominic's curiosity was piqued. What could the congressman possibly have to speak with him about? *He must want me to hook him up with some medical program in his congressional district or something.* "Sure. I can stop by."

"Excellent. I will leave the details with your assistant." He nodded as Sylvia signaled to him from across the room. "I must leave. I look forward to speaking with you later." Dominic watched him strut across the hospital lobby to his entourage and leave the hospital en masse.

~~~

Michael walked up to Dominic as he stood on the fringes of the crowd, observing the moving and shaking. "Dr. Bastille. I'm glad you could join us." He held out his hand.

Dominic shook it. "Thanks for inviting me."

"Could I have a word with you privately, please?" Michael escorted Dominic to a quiet balcony that overlooked the Atlanta skyline. They both stood at the ledge and looked down upon the moving, sparkling displays and throngs of people below.

"I remember you from The Porter Foundation

fundraiser. You were accompanied by Taryn."

Dominic swirled his bourbon in his hand as he tried to keep the jealousy from his voice. "You know Taryn?"

Amusement danced in Michael's liquid brown eyes at Dominic's tone. "I do. We knew each other quite well at one point. But of course, you already know this?" He sipped his scotch and eyed Dominic over the rim of his glass.

Dominic clenched his jaw at the thought of Taryn with another man--especially this one. "She may have mentioned it."

Michael snorted. "I can assure you she did not, at least voluntarily. It was not a pleasant time for her." He looked at Dominic curiously. "But that is not the source of your animosity."

Dominic blinked in surprise. "Excuse me?"

"Dr. Bastille, a large part of being a politician involves being able to read people. A successful politician does it well, and I am quite successful. This is not conceit or arrogance, but fact. And I can tell that something about Taryn is weighing on you heavily."

"I don't see how that's any of your business."

"Ah, but Taryn is my business, in a friendly way. Though our relationship ended years ago, I make it a point to keep apprised of her welfare. I owe her that much." Seeing Dominic's curious expression, Michael continued his explanation. "Taryn is a gifted game developer, computer programmer, et cetera, and very good at what she does. I have been around enough Silicon Valley techies to know. Yet she remains in that world but not of it; doing so keeps her sane.

"Our relationship was more a testament to my perseverance than any grand passion. I was newly elected to the state assembly and was drunk with victory and my own sense of possibility. When the beautiful, brilliant, talented, and principled Taryn was recommended to me in order to create political simulations for my campaign, and proceeded to turn down my invitations to dinner, the theatre, to wine tastings in Napa and Sonoma, I was determined to have her. I persuaded some people I knew to hire Taryn on some freelance projects. Again, Taryn had the requisite skill set and vision; those that hired her were not disappointed in her work, which led to more work. What holds true for politics is also true for other aspects of life: it isn't just what you know, but who you know." He stared down into his drink, lost in memory. "I was not kind to her. I justified my...solicitations of donations, shall we say--especially private ones--and favor exchanges as simply a byproduct of my political achievements. As my just due. My greed took its toll on our relationship, which was already precarious due to my frequent travels. I persuaded Taryn to abandon her principles—to not speak of what her simulations were being modified to do, which was far from their original purpose--for what she thought might be love, and she paid a dear price for it. For that matter, so did I."

"Well, it's not the first time that Taryn abandoned her principles." As soon as the words came out of his mouth, Dominic regretted them.

Michael laughed. "Taryn? Are you serious?" Seeing the look on Dominic's face, Michael exclaimed, "*Por Dios*, you are! Dr. Bastille, surely you do not believe what is written in the media? Or what you are told, perhaps by parties with a certain agenda, *¿verdad?*"

Dominic again tried to feign ignorance. "What are you talking about, Congressman?"

A knowing smile played across Michael's full lips. "I could not help but notice, at the fundraiser, that you were paid quite a lot of attention by a Miss Cecily Porter?"

"So?"

"I also noticed that the attention was not mutual. Indeed, the bulk of your attention was devoted to Taryn. I continued to notice that this did not please Miss Porter in the least. She is the head of the Public Relations department for your transplant center, is she not? And, rumor has it, your ex-fiancée?"

"Very few people know about that at Atlanta Transplant Consortium, and I'd like to keep it that way."

Michael inclined his head in agreement. "Of course. It is not my intention to put your personal affairs, as my younger constituents say, on blast. My sources are discreet, and impeccable. Surely you didn't think that my tour of your transplant center and laboratory were merely window dressing? I meant what I said, that I am interested in your research as it concerns my constituents, many of whom are lower-income and would languish longer than normal on an organ transplant list. But that is another discussion for another time." Michael waved his free hand in dismissal. "Let's get back to the matter at hand. Who told you that Taryn had been awarded her freelance projects in California on a less than honorable basis?"

Dominic hesitated. "Cecily," he admitted.

"And she did this out of the kindness of her heart? As a means of looking out for your welfare?"

Michael's sarcasm was not lost on Dominic, and he cursed himself for believing Cecily for even a second.

But she was nothing if not persuasive, the Queen of Spin; she could have given any politician a run for their money. But she'd sounded so sure, and there were those articles, and Cecily's claim that she'd spoken to some of these people, including the Congressman... "Wait a minute. Did Cecily speak to you about Taryn?"

Michael sipped his drink. "She called my office and spoke with my campaign manager, Sylvia, who is also my fiancée. Sylvia has her own jealous streak and has not been a fan of

Taryn's since she and I began dating years ago. I am not proud to say that I cheated on Taryn with Sylvia, and Sylvia has never quite forgiven me—or herself—for playing second fiddle during that time."

"Well, she's obviously forgiven you. You're engaged now."

Michael shrugged. "An engagement ring only solicits a certain amount of forgiveness. Sylvia will always second-guess my actions and motives, especially since Taryn will always hold a special place in my heart. That is no way to live, or to love. But she will do, for now. Being perceived as having a steady relationship is helpful in getting elected."

*Ohhhkay.* Dominic was not even trying to get caught up in the congressman's love drama, so he switched the subject back to Taryn. "So basically, you're saying that Sylvia played up Taryn's media-driven links to her previous lawsuit, and some of her previous freelance projects, in an effort to get back at Taryn because you still have feelings for her."

Michael smirked and raised his scotch in a salute. "*Felicitaciones*, Dr. Bastille. I think you have solved your mystery. Although it wasn't much of one."

"Given the turn this conversation has taken, you can call me Nick."

"And you may call me Mikey. Only Taryn ever called me that," he chuckled. "I thought it irritating at the time, as if I were an eight year-old boy. But now, through the clear vision of hindsight, I find it endearing."

"How about Mike?

"Much better for a grown man, don't you think?" The two men exchanged a laugh before Michael's tone turned serious. "Nick, I have told you all this because I would like for you to learn from my mistakes. Taryn is not a toy to be played with, then placed upon a shelf once you've grown tired. She is a treasure to be savored. I can tell that you are in love with her, even if you have not yet admitted it to yourself. That being said, if you have made a mistake, own up to it. Fight for her. Do what I did not, and have regretted ever since." At that moment Sylvia came over and whispered in Michael's ear. "I must take my leave of you, Nick." He retrieved a business card from his inner jacket pocket and scribbled on the back of it. "My personal cell phone number is on the back. Feel free to call anytime. In the meantime, perhaps you will think about visiting a hospital in my area, as a possible location for you to expand your research. As my guest, of course."

Dominic took the card and placed it in his own pocket, then gave the congressman his own card in exchange. "Send me the particulars and I'll see what I can do."

Michael nodded his head and followed Sylvia into the crowd. Dominic drank the last of his bourbon and thought of the monumental mess he'd made with Taryn, accusing her of using the interview as a springboard into his life, as a means of trying to get her claws into him and the what some may perceive as a Bastille fortune. How was he going to fix it?

~~~

Taryn fiddled around with the script for a new role-playing game, but her heart wasn't in it. She'd even opted to work from home because she wasn't in the mood to deal with a lot of people. She had a very capable staff; they could handle most issues that arose.

She rose and padded into the kitchen. She wasn't

really hungry, but she just felt like doing something that wasn't work related. Taryn pulled a jar of peanut butter and a box of crackers from the cabinet, made herself a snack, only to push it away after a couple of bites of a peanut butter-smeared cracker. She wandered into the living room and powered up her flatscreen TV with her smartwatch. Not even back episodes of *Game of Thrones* could hold her interest. She shuffled back upstairs to her bedroom and flopped face down upon the bed before finally crawling beneath the covers.

She knew what was happening. She'd been through a similar episode back in California, when her career was almost over before it began--all because she trusted the wrong person. Taryn curled up in the fetal position and remembered the grueling trial, the attempts by Cameron--the defendant--to portray her as a stereotypical geek girl, socially awkward and latching on to the first sign of affection given. He'd even intimated that Taryn only got projects because she was pretty and had breasts--conveniently omitting the fact that she had not one, but two *cum laude* master's degrees from Berkeley and fairly high government security clearance, as required when working on military-grade government projects. She would be forever grateful to Michael for hooking her up with that attorney, although it was the least he could have done after tipping out on her with Sylvia. Still, that had been Taryn's lowest point of her career--maybe even her life. Until now.

Taryn turned her face into the pillow and let the tears fall. Her professional livelihood was at stake because she threw caution to the winds. As much as she wanted to blame Cecily, Taryn knew that it was her own fault for getting involved with a client--again. And what did she have to show for it? An ex-man who thought she was a conniving gold digger--or better yet, a whore who exchanged dates for job perks.

Taryn rolled onto her back and let the tears course into her temples. At least she still had her work. Despite Dominic's feelings about her personally, even he couldn't deny that her medical holograms were some of her best work ever. He should get a lot of awards and shine because of it; not that he'd think to thank her for them. Since Taryn already owned the patent for her particular type of technology, she wasn't worried about anyone trying to steal it this time. In fact, if she really wanted to be petty, she could block Dominic from using any of her work. Granted, she'd have to refund the money paid to MacSim for the project, but Dominic would have to start his research all over, and he probably wouldn't get anything half as good as what she'd created. Not to mention, word had already started to get out about Taryn's next-level work on Dominic's research project; she'd have no shortage of potential, deep-pocketed clients clamoring for her services. It would serve Dominic right, after the way he'd treated her.

She turned her head into the pillow and cried some more. What was she going to do?

~~~

Taryn woke up the next morning with swollen eyes and a congested chest. Her body reacted to intense stress in the form of colds, which always took up residence in her lungs. Sleeping with the air conditioner on "high" probably didn't help either. She called the office, found out that everything was still kosher, and told them she was taking the day off so as not to infect everyone else.

"Oh, Taryn, you keep getting calls from Dr. Dominic Bastille," Petra, her second-in-command, said. "He kept getting your voicemail, he said, and hadn't gotten a reply to his emails, so he got someone to patch him through to me. You want his info?"

"No, I already have it, Petra, thanks. Actually, can you do me a favor? I'll send his info to you, along with a summary of the project completion. If you could contact him and make sure he has no further questions about the beta product, then send him the final invoice--it's in the system--I'd appreciate it."

"On it, boss lady. What if he wants to talk to you?"

"I'm out of pocket to all clients until I lick this cold. But if any clients ask, I'm simply out of the office and unavailable. Call me if anything crucial happens, like the building is on fire or Steve Jobs comes back from the grave for a chat."

Petra laughed. "Will do. Feel better."

Later that day her cell phone rang, and she barely had the energy to answer it. "Hello," Taryn croaked.

"What the hell is wrong with you?" Sheridan demanded in alarm. "You sound like Bea Arthur."

"Hey, I liked Bea Arthur, God rest her. She was great on *Maude* and *The Golden Girls*."

"Seriously, what's wrong?"

"Just a cold. I'll be fine."

"Sounds like more than a cold. What are you taking for it?"

"The cold is a stress reaction; you know how I do. I'm taking hot tea spiked with ginger, lemon, honey, and bourbon; and pineapple juice."

"That's it? That's all you're taking? You need an antibiotic."

"Colds are caused by viruses, so antibiotics won't

work. What kind of doctor are you?" Taryn teased.

"The kind that knows an upper respiratory infection when she hears one."

Taryn started to respond but a coughing fit momentarily robbed her of speech.

"I don't like the way you sound at all, Taryn." Sheridan's voice was filled with both personal and professional concern. "You need to go see a doctor, stat."

Taryn took a sip of now-cold tea. "I'll be fine, Sherry. I took the day off."

"Wonders never cease, I guess. But make sure you don't do any work. You know how you like to fiddle with unfinished projects when you're allegedly off the clock. Having a home office isn't good for your health."

"Trust, I don't have the energy to fiddle with anything. In fact, I think I'm going go back to bed."

"You do that. And when you wake up, you go to a doctor, or urgent care center, or somewhere with licensed medical professionals who can write you a prescription."

"I've been through this before. I'll kick this in a few days."

Sheridan was unconvinced, but any further argument would be wasted effort. Taryn was stubborn; she wouldn't go to a doctor unless she was bleeding from her eye sockets. "Well, get some rest, and try not to cough up a lung. I'll check on you later."

"Ha ha. Holla atcha later."

In her office in Philadelphia, Sheridan Bastille disconnected the call and tapped her cell phone against her chin, thinking. She pressed one of her pre-programmed keys to place another call.

~~~

The buzzing of her doorbell synchronized with the flashing display of her smartwatch. Taryn rolled over with a groan and tapped the screen of her cellphone, which lay atop the wireless charger. The security camera display showed a figure laden with plastic grocery bags, fidgeting impatiently beneath the camera over the front porch. Taryn squinted her sleep-encrusted eyes; the figure looked a lot like Dominic Bastille.

She rolled out of bed and stumbled downstairs as the doorbell gave another angry peal. "Hold your horses," she mumbled as she approached the door. She looked at the interior camera display to make sure it really was Dominic, then unlocked the door. "Yes?" she rasped.

"You sound terrible." Dominic pushed past her and headed toward the kitchen. One of the plastic grocery bags grazed Taryn's bare leg.

Taryn entered the kitchen to find Dominic

unpacking his bags, storing some things the refrigerator, and other in the cabinets. Taryn crossed her arms across her chest and tried not to feel so elated at his presence. "Why are you here?"

"Sheridan called me." He opened a jar of chicken soup and dumped its contents in a large plastic bowl that was resting in the dish drainer by the sink. He stuck the bowl in the microwave and set the timer for three minutes.

"Well, you can go now. Thanks for the groceries."

"I'm not leaving until I see for myself what's wrong with you, since you seem to have an aversion to doctors."

"Just one," Taryn snapped.

The microwaved dinged and Dominic removed the steaming-hot bowl of soup. "I deserve that," he said as he placed the bowl atop the counter.

"Yeah, you do."

Dominic turned to face Taryn. "Look I messed up, alright? I shouldn't have listened to Cecily. I should have believed you. I was wrong."

"Well, you're a day late and a dollar short."

Dominic sighed and ran a hand across the top of his head. "Look, can we call a truce? I just want to make sure you're okay. Sheridan said you might have an upper respiratory infection."

"Sheridan needs to mind her own beeswax." Taryn fell into another fit of coughing.

Dominic frowned as he grabbed a glass from the dish drainer and filled it with water from the spigot on the refrigerator door. "In case you've forgotten, Sheridan considers anyone she loves as her business. So, you're stuck with me for the time being." He handed Taryn the glass. "Now drink some of that and let me listen to your lungs."

Taryn drained half the glass and sat down at the kitchen table. Dominic retrieved his stethoscope from a leather bag that Taryn hadn't seen. He rubbed the bell of the stethoscope with his palm to warm it, then placed it against the thin cotton fabric of Taryn's T-shirt. He tried not to pay attention to the hardened, braless nipples poking through the logo on the front of the shirt . "Take a deep breath," he instructed. "Again." After a few respirations and listening to the back and front of her chest, Dominic removed the stethoscope from his ears and tucked it back into his bag. He ran his fingers under her jaw and felt her swollen lymph nodes, then felt her forehead with the back of his hand. "Where's your pharmacy? I'm calling in a prescription. Are you allergic to any medications?"

Taryn shook her head as a wave of weariness washed over her. "No allergies. What's wrong?"

"Sheridan was right about an upper respiratory infection. You have bronchitis. If left untreated, it could develop into pneumonia." He fished his cell phone out of his pocket. "Pharmacy?"

Taryn pointed to a refrigerator magnet from her local chain drugstore, which contained all of the pertinent store information. Dominic gave the pharmacy his name, DEA number, medication, dosage, and Taryn's information before hanging up. "It'll be ready in half an hour. I'll go pick it up. In the meantime, you need to get some rest." He looked at the cooling soup on the counter. "Are you hungry?"

Taryn shook her head. Food was the last thing on her mind. She just wanted to sleep.

"When as the last time you ate?" At Taryn's shrug, Dominic said, "Well, can you force a bit of that soup down? You need the fluids. Then you can go to sleep."

Taryn watched with weary eyes as Dominic poured some of the soup into a large mug, then placed the mug in front of her. "Drink that down, then I'll help you upstairs."

"I can make it upstairs myself." Taryn's voice sounded petulant, even to her own ears.

"Fine. Drink that down, and you can go upstairs by yourself, then."

Taryn was in no mood to argue. She managed to drink the soup down before the mug became too heavy for her to lift. She staggered to her feet, and Dominic snaked an arm around her waist to steady her. Without commentary, Dominic escorted Taryn upstairs to her bedroom. Even in her fever-induced fog, Taryn had to admit to herself that it was nice to have someone to lean on, even if just for a little while. Ryan, who turned into a big baby over a paper cut, would have bathed himself in hand sanitizer before disappearing until she recovered. She crawled beneath the sheets and was asleep by the time Dominic pulled the comforter over her body.

~~~

Taryn opened her eyes and was surprised to find the room in darkness; the only illumination came from a nearby street light. *How long have I been asleep?* She was breathing through her mouth because her nose was so stopped up. She sat up and pushed back the lightweight comforter. Even that small movement made her want to lie back down and sleep some more.

"How are you feeling?"

Taryn jumped and screamed as much as her congested lungs would allow, which wasn't much. Her heart pounded as she fumbled to turn on her bedside lamp. Dominic sat in the corner chair in her bedroom; he placed his tablet on the arm of the chair and approached the bed, stethoscope in hand.

"What...how..." Taryn rasped.

"I put a piece of paper in the lock before I left to pick up your prescription," he admitted with a sheepish glance. "I didn't want to have to wake you up to let me back in. Of course, if you had regular keys like normal people, I wouldn't have had to take such drastic measures."

Taryn tried to chuckle at Dominic's teasing. "Metal keys and locks are old school. You need to get with the future."

"Not if the future will keep me from getting into my own house." Dominic walked back to the chair and retrieved a brownish-orange plastic medication bottle. He unscrewed the white top a shook out a large white pill. "Here you go," he said as he handed it to Taryn, along with a glass of water that was on the nightstand. "Amoxicillin. Take three times a day until it's all gone, even if you feel better. Don't skip any doses."

"Mm hmm," Taryn grunted as she swallowed the pill with water. She replaced the glass on the nightstand and flopped back against the pillows, spent.

Dominic's heart turned over at how vulnerable she looked, breathing through her mouth because her chest and nose were so congested. The epiphany hit him like a ton of bricks: he was in love with Taryn, was tired of his life without her in it, and didn't want to spend another day without her.

Taryn cracked open her eyes and saw Dominic staring at her. "You're still here?"

"I'm still here."

"Good." Taryn curled up beneath the covers, even though it was over seventy degrees inside the room. She fell back asleep almost immediately.

Later on that night, Taryn awoke with no fever and feeling slightly hungry. As he did earlier, Dominic jumped up from the corner chair when he noticed she was awake. "Hey, how are you feeling?" He felt her forehead and neck again, then took another listen with his stethoscope.

"Better. The antibiotics are already working. I'm actually a bit hungry."

"Well, your fever's gone and your lungs sound clearer." He rose and placed the stethoscope on the nightstand. "I've got some more soup for you, and another dose of meds." He gave Taryn another pill.

"What are you, my pusher?" she grumbled as she

swallowed it and made a face at the slightly bitter aftertaste.

Dominic's lips quirked up in a half-smile. "Something like that. And you must be feeling better if you can make smartass comments."

"Whatever."

Dominic chuckled. "Be back with your soup."

Dominic returned with a tray bearing two steaming bowls of chicken soup and a tall glass of orange juice. Taryn sat up and Dominic settled the tray across her lap. She dove into the soup, suddenly ravenous, while Dominic ate at a more sedate pace.

"Don't you have a job to be at?" Taryn asked around a spoonful of soup. "People to cut?"

Dominic sat on the side of the bed and ate his soup from the tray as well. "One of the perks of being in charge is the ability to take leave if need be, so I'm good."

Taryn scraped the bottom of her empty bowl, trying to decide who to kill first when she felt up to it: Sheridan or Dominic. "Sheridan shouldn't have called you."

"I disagree." Dominic took the empty dishes back to the kitchen and returned with a cup of hot tea. "No bourbon," he announced. "Doctor's orders."

Taryn wrapped her hands around the mug for

warmth. "Well, thank you. For everything."

"I'm glad to do it." He settled back in the chair and debated on whether or not to bring up his next question. *In for a penny, in for a pound.* "Sheridan also mentioned that you get sick like this when you're overly stressed." He sighed and stared down at his hands "I apologize for my part in that."

Taryn frowned. "Sheridan really needs to stay out of my beeswax  sometimes."

"Good luck with that. I've been trying since birth and it hasn't happened yet." Dominic sighed deeply. A large part of this was his fault. He knew that Cecily had a vindictive streak, and he should have neutralized her from the beginning. Not to mention, he'd falsely accused Taryn and risked losing her. "I'm in love with you," he blurted.

"Good for you."  Taryn placed the tea on her nightstand and leaned back against the pillows.

"We can make this work, Taryn."

"How? You don't trust me and you don't care if Cecily sows her seeds of destruction, as
long as she arranges good media coverage for your career."

*Ouch.* "Look, I admit that I messed up by jumping to conclusions..."

"Jumping to conclusions?" Taryn snarled. "Sherlock Holmes jumped to conclusions. You made leaps that would do an Olympic hurdler proud."

"Be that as it may, I'm apologizing for believing the spin against you. I knew how Cecily could be, and I let things get out of hand because it was easier than trying to shut her down. I'm sorry." He reached over and grabbed her hand. "I want us to try again, for real this time. I love you. Can we try, Taryn? Please?"

"I don't know. I just don't see how this could work, what with me being a whore for projects and all."

"I told you I was sorry, and I apologized for my error in judgment. What more do you want me to say?"

"Nothing, Dominic. I think you've said enough."

"Fine." Dominic rose and removed his car keys from his pocket. "Take the next dose of your medication in six hours. Instructions are on the bottle. There's another jar of soup in the cabinet, and juice in the fridge. Hope you feel better soon."

Taryn watched as he left the room. Seconds later, she heard his car start, then fade away as he pulled out of the driveway. She'd won the battle, but the hollow feeling inside made Taryn wonder if she'd lost the war. She curled up beneath the covers and went back to sleep, so that she wouldn't have to think about it.

~~~

"What the fuck is your problem?"

Taryn's eyebrows rose at Sheridan's irate tone. Her friend had checked in on her every day for the past four days and while those calls had been full of concern, this call was obviously taking a different tack. "Excuse me?"

"You are not excused," Sheridan snarled. "What the fuck did you do to Dominic?"

"What? I didn't do anything."

"Then explain to me why he's gone incognegro all of a sudden. He goes to work, comes home, goes off the grid. No one has heard from him, not even Mark."

"What makes you think I had anything to do with it?"

"Because I know about his error in accusing you falsely. And because I know you, Taryn. You nurse grudges for eons. And chances are that if Dominic tried to come correct, you shot him down." Taryn's silence on the other end spoke volumes, so Sheridan pressed further. "Well?"

Taryn flopped back against her pillows. "He told me he was in love with me, Sheridan."

"And that's a bad thing?"

"He didn't mean it, Sherry. He just said that to get

back into my good graces, like I was some twit who would wipe the slate clean after hearing that."

"The man drove over thirty minutes in rush-hour traffic to bring you chicken soup and juice. That's love."

"Whatever."

"And for the record, I have no recollection of him saying 'I love you' to any woman who was not a blood relative. Ever. Not even Cecily."

"But they were engaged. How could he not love her?"

"Do I really need to answer that? People have gotten married for less."

"Well, he should be thrilled at the turn of events. No man wants to be with a money-grubbing whore."

Sheridan sighed as she chose her next words carefully. "Taryn, you have to learn to let shit go. Standing on principle is all well and good, and I admire you for it. But pride won't keep you warm at night. Case in point: you could be tended to by your own personal, board-certified surgeon right about now; instead, you're hugged up under the covers in that computer house, all by your damn self. Not even a goldfish for company. How is that helping anything?"

Taryn wasn't in the mood for Sheridan's logic, which was uncomfortably sound. "I'm about to go back to sleep; I'm tired."

"Uh huh. Well before you go, let me leave you with something to sleep on. One: my brother has managed to avoid being locked down for over thirty-nine years, yet he is giving you the handcuffs and the keys. Second: you are my best friend, Taryn, and I love you, but Dominic is my brother. I will fuck you up if you hurt him over some bullshit."

"Better pack a lunch if you try, but duly noted."

"I don't sell wolf tickets. Now, get some rest and I'll holler at you tomorrow." She disconnected the call without so much as a goodbye.

Taryn replaced her smartphone upon the nightstand and lay back against the pillows, thinking.

~~~

A knock on his office door interrupted Dominic's concentration. His work had been his salvation for the past five days, and he was loathe to leave its protective bubble. Before he could answer, the door opened and Lori entered. "Yes, Lori?"

"You have a visitor."

"Tell them I'm unavailable."

"I think you'd want to see them."

"If it's yet another group of interest from Vincent, I'm not in the mood to play tour guide."

Lori shook her head. "No groups, no Vincent."

Dominic sighed and leaned back in his chair. He rubbed a hand across the beginnings of stubble on his face and felt weary. "Fine. Send them in, but buzz me in ten minutes with some sort of emergency. They won't be staying long."

Lori nodded and exited. Dominic closed his eyes and pinched the bridge of his nose in attempt to stave off an impending headache that was lurking behind his forehead.

"Hi."

Dominic's eyes flew open at the sound of the slightly congested voice. Taryn stood there, layered in a sweatshirt and T-shirt. Her locs were pulled back into a ponytail and her jeans had holes in the knees that were accidentally fashionable. "Hi."

"I won't take up too much of your time; I know you're busy."

Dominic eyed the dark circles beneath her eyes, and her drawn face. "You shouldn't be out of bed. Pushing yourself could cause a serious setback. Bronchitis is no joke."

"I know, but I needed to say this."

"You could have called."

"Would you have answered?"

Dominic inclined his head in acknowledgement and continued to stare at her.

Taryn shifted her Converse-shod feet; she had to get this off her chest, and she hadn't expected Dominic to even see her, let alone make things easy for her. Still, she found his stare disconcerting. And wary. "I came to apologize. For how I acted the other day, and for what I said."

Dominic stared at her for a few seconds more. "Apology accepted." He picked up some papers on his desk and began reading.

Taryn continued to stand, at a loss as for what to do next. While she hadn't expected a warm greeting, she also hadn't expected Dominic to totally freeze her out.

Dominic looked up from his papers. "Was there something else that you needed?"

The chill in his voice gave Taryn pause, but she forged ahead. "I was hoping that we could discuss this like adults."

"Oh, so now you want to act like an adult?" Dominic's detached façade crumbled and he let his hurt and anger seep through. "I think the term you used was 'a day late and a dollar short'."

"So we're not going to talk about this at all? You're going to stay mad at me?"

"Why not? It seems to work well for you."

Taryn nodded at the accurate zinger. "Alright. I deserved that."

"Yeah, you do. And to answer your previous question, what is there to talk about? I tell you I'm in love with you and your reply is, 'Good for you.' I apologize for judging you unfairly, you tell me that it's a wasted effort. I can't win for losing with you, so why bother? Life is too short to stay where I'm not wanted."

Taryn broke into deep, rasping sobs, even as part of her was horrified at the display of emotion. She sank into one of the chairs facing his desk. "I can't do this, Dominic! I can't. I wake up every morning, and I can't breathe! I can't breathe because you aren't there. And I tried to stop loving you. It's been weeks and I still can't stop loving you. And when I take a moment to stop and question my sanity for still loving you, the thought of it makes me happy! It brings me peace. And I'm sorry that's not enough for you." She ended with shuddering, incoherent sobs.

Dominic rushed from behind his desk to take Taryn into his arms. It was like coming home. "Shhh, shhh," he whispered as he crouched beside the chair and rocked her in his arms. Just the sound of her sobs brought tears to his own eyes. When her crying subsided to a less frantic level, he cradled her damp face in his hands. "Taryn, for the past five days, I have been in hell. I do my surgeries, I sit in meetings, and it's like I'm in a box. When I got calls from medical journals and medical schools about the holographic simulations, the first person I thought to call was you. Not my twin sister, not my dad or my other brothers and sisters, not Mark, but you," his voice broke, "and I couldn't.

"I was stupid, and I panicked because I was afraid of loving you so much. I was stupid, and said some things I shouldn't have said. and I've regretted it ever since. So I'm asking you, Taryn, to please, please ride this with me till the wheels fall off."

Taryn smiled through fresh tears. "Five days?"

"Five days, fourteen hours, and twelve minutes. Not that I've kept track."

Taryn and Dominic shared a laugh, and it felt good. They sat in comfortable silence, listening to each other's heartbeats, interrupted by an occasional cough from Taryn. Dominic kissed Taryn's ponytailed locs and asked, "So?"

Taryn looked up in confusion. "So, what?"

"Will you give me another chance? Will you ride

with me until the wheels fall off?"

"Only if I get to replace the navigation system with a computerized one."

Dominic threw back his head in laughter. Taryn joined in, and the two sounds joined to make an even sweeter one.

## About the Author

TIFFANY M. DAVIS is an award-winning writer whose work has appeared on Medium, Black Girl Nerds, Vixen Varsity, and in *QBR: The Black Book Review*; as well as the anthologies *Malaria Shots Not Included* and *One Day I Woke Up and Put My Crown On: the Project of 76 Voices*. A graduate of Georgetown University in Washington, DC who was trained as a chef at the Culinary Institute of America in Hyde Park, NY, she currently resides in the Atlanta, GA area.

Web: www.tiffscribes.com
Blog: tiffscribes.wordpress.com
Facebook: Facebook.com/tiffscribes
Twitter: @tiffscribes
Instagram: tiffscribes